Contents

Robert Westall

A Walk on the Wild Side

mammoth

First published in Great Britain 1989
by Methuen Children's Books Ltd
'The Creatures in the House' and
'A Walk on the Wild Side' were first published
in *The Haunting of Chas McGill*
by Robert Westall, Macmillan 1982
Mandarin paperback edition published 1991
Reissued 1998 by Mammoth
an imprint of Egmont Children's Books Limited
Michelin House, 81 Fulham Road, London SW3 6RB

ISBN 0 7497 0147 1

10 9 8 7 6 5 4 3 2 1

A CIP catalogue record for this title
is available from the British Library

Printed in Great Britain
by Cox & Wyman Ltd, Reading, Berkshire

CONTENTS

To Geoffrey, my cat, who with a paw-print on a letter set this book in motion.

BUTTONS

Considering their final battle, it's odd that Buttons the cat and Kerry Turnbull, the Australian millionaire, should have arrived in my life on the same day.

Mind you, we didn't call the cat Buttons at first. Just 'that damned kitten'. He had to earn his name and his fame.

He was brought to my door early one October evening by Scott Walker, a thirteen-year-old with time on his hands, a bike, a pair of very sharp eyes and a heart big enough to enfold every stray cat in the village. It caused Scott problems at home and when the problems got too big, he brought them to me. A total sucker where cats are concerned, his sharp eyes had soon spotted a fellow sufferer.

The doorbell rang as I was getting dressed for the cricket league annual general meeting and hot-pot supper. (I'm the captain of the local team, Preston Green.) I went down in my stockinged feet, and there was Scott with another scrap of underfed fur clinging to his jumper.

This particular scrap of fur turned and looked me straight in the eye, from a distance of about half a metre. That's unusual because, for cats, eyeball to eyeball is the ultimate threat-challenge. But Buttons' gaze was not threatening. It had that world-weary watchfulness only achieved by streetwise teenagers and elderly Catholic priests. It assessed me without hope or fear; it read my soul and found me a sucker. After that, there was nothing to do but take him. Protests, about having four cats already, froze on my lips. It was lucky I had an understanding wife and lots of outbuildings.

I confess I took Buttons straight through to my wife in the kitchen and forgot him, and went eagerly to the

7

hot-pot supper. It's always a jolly occasion to mark the end of the season, and gives the secretaries a chance to sort out the balls-ups in next year's fixture lists. But that year I went with extra eagerness, because Gunton C.C. had been taken over by Kerry Turnbull. He'd acquired Gunton Manor as a greenfield site for his new computer complex, and having one green field to spare, he'd offered it to Gunton Cricket Club. (Having first made Harry Coe, Gunton's captain, into his head gardener.)

It was an offer poor Harry couldn't possibly refuse. But miracles were promised. A pitch like a billiard table; an electronic scoreboard that would give every player a print-out at the end of the game at the touch of a button; brand new changing rooms with needle showers; and a full-time groundsman. Even professional sightscreens made by the same firm that made them for Lord's.

There were some reckoned Gunton were selling their birthright for a mess of pottage. But the only mess involved, said others, was the Gunton of old. They played on their village green, which sounds idyllic. If you forgot the coke cans and the crisp bags and the dog dirt you trod in while trying to take a catch at deep mid-on. Their pavilion had originally been built to house convalescent soldiers from the First World War, and was only kept waterproof with tarred brown paper. The only reason we tolerated Gunton was that they always cheerfully occupied the bottom of the league table, which saved the rest of us that particuliar humiliation . . .

Kerry Turnbull was keen to make friends, that first year. The hot-pot supper's normally held in the Mayston Arms at Mayston. But Kerry offered us a free nosh-up in his staff dining room at the Manor, so we took him up on it.

Beforehand, we duly inspected the new miracles. The pitch was as green, smooth and striped as the picture on a packet of lawn fertiliser. The sightscreens did have the Famous Name engraved on small brass plates at the bottom. And the electronic scoreboard glowed up red in the dusk, to wish us good evening, at the touch of a button. Some attendant creep whispered that Kerry had designed the scoreboard himself, and even the Oval had nothing like it.

The meal, in the mahogany-tabled air-conditioned dining room, would not have shamed the West End. But not by any stretch of the imagination could it have been called hot-pot . . .

Then our host himself got up to make a short speech of welcome. He was, to say the least, intimidating. Six foot six, I judged, in his stockinged feet. Broad as a barn. All of sixteen stones without an ounce of surplus flesh. A face whose bones had a thick brutality that was only redeemed from Neanderthal Manhood by the smallest, quickest and coldest grey eyes I've ever seen. Not for nothing was he called the Great White Shark of the mini-computer trade.

After a few polite trivialities, he only said two things. That their name would be changed from Gunton C.C. to Gunton Manor C.C. and that he hoped they would make their mark on the league next season . . . But it seemed to send a shudder down a lot of spines. I had the feeling that the league which we'd found such fun would never be the same again.

On the way home, people blustered a lot, trying to cheer themselves up. They called Gunton 'a rich man's toy' and Kerry 'a rabbit who had bought himself a place in the team'. But they were whistling in the dark.

Kerry didn't look like a rabbit to me.

He looked horribly like an Aussie fast bowler.

When I got home, Buttons was sitting neatly in my wife's lap. He gave me a look of cool pity; as if I had missed my chance to be first in his heart.

My wife said, 'This kitten's worked out that the hand that wields the tin-opener rules the world. He's cadged a whole tin of tuna out of me.' She grinned with absurd delight at her own weakness.

'Shall I take him out to the stable with the others?' I said. I suppose I was vaguely jealous, as well as being annoyed about the price of tuna. My wife likes cats, but she's not normally a pushover.

9

'Oh, *no!*' she said. 'It's too cold. There could be a frost tonight, and he's too little. I think he'd better come up to bed with us, so I can keep an eye on him.'

'Cats are not allowed in the bedroom! Cats are not allowed in the *house!*' I was outraged. Still upset by Kerry Turnbull, I was ready for a row.

But Buttons seemed somehow to understand. He jumped down from my wife's knee, stumbling a little with weakness. Then sniffed at my wife's knitting bag that hung from the back of her chair. Gave a pathetic little leap, clawed up the bag and settled inside among the wool. Fast asleep in a minute, on his back, feet in the air and face composed in that prim satisfied smirk that cats have when they're asleep upside down.

I thought my wife would go berserk; she's a passionate knitter. But she just said, in a cooing voice, 'He's come a long journey, that one. Alone. And he's so *little.*'

I should have been warned then. Should have put my foot down. But it was her knitting bag, and I suppose I hoped he'd disgrace himself and bring her to her senses.

How wrong I was. I still didn't realise I'd met my *second* empire-builder of the day.

At breakfast-time, my daughters were a pushover too. First he was in Fiona's lap, then he was in Sarah's. Before they went to school they were fighting for his favours, trying to lure him back with offers of bacon rind held surreptitiously under the table. When they had gone, he was back in my wife's lap. And by the time I went to work he was in our charlady's lap, as she drank her revving-up mug of tea with three sugars. He seemed to have the power to drive the average female bananas. I suppose I could see why; he was little, he was thin and frail, and he had these enormous dark eyes. What I reckoned was a bit scary was that he *knew* he was frail, and used it as a weapon. In our welfare state, frailty is the strongest weapon of all. There is a mallard with a broken wing which hangs around Scoresby Mere down the road. I used to feel sorry for it, before I realised it was the fattest mallard on the mere. Every passing holiday-maker made sure *it* got enough . . .

Anyway, Buttons stayed with us and ate everything they threw at him, and grew very fast. Until he reached the last stage of kittenhood – the adolescent long-legged stage. And there he stuck, as winter passed. Wife and daughters fretted, as he failed to grow any more, failed to put on weight. I had to take him to the vet, though I protested that his nose was cold, his eyes bright, and he was forever on the move, nosing out new trouble.

'Stray, is he?' asked the vet. 'Left his mother too young. Half-starved. Missed his growing time. He'll not grow any more now. But he's fit enough. Nice-looking cat – could be a pedigree – an Oriental Red. You've done well to get him for nowt.' He, too, was cuddling and playing with the cunning little sod. And he was usually a hard bloke, a farming vet really . . .

I looked at Buttons again; I suppose scales of familiarity fell off my eyes. He had been a kind of fawn when he first came, dull with the dirt of travel. Now, his coat shone like soft cream and silver silk. All but the deep pink ridge down his back, pink rims to his ears, and the strengthening pink rings that ran down his tail to the rose-pink tip. He still looked frail, but beautiful. Not at all feminine, but delicately masculine, a little dandy with those huge dark eyes that held such depths of knowing.

He looked back at me with that old cool assessing tolerance. He knew that mine was one heart he'd still failed to collect, and I think it irked him slightly.

One of the sad things is that kittens develop so many gifts that they lose later. Kittens can run sideways and backwards, like crabs. Kittens can leap vertically into the air like Hawker Harriers, when under attack. Kittens can climb curtains, slowly, hand over hand or rather paw over paw. I suppose they find no use for these skills as they grow up, and let them lapse as they sink into heavy middle age. But Buttons was much too wily to throw away such gifts. It was a treat to watch him climb a two-metre larch-lap fence thoughtfully and slowly, like an experienced alpinist. It got him attention; it also got him safety. One morning, when I was weeding the rose bed, I saw him go up very quickly and crouch on top. A minute later, a huge Alsation came blundering into my garden, nose to ground. He went right to the bottom of the fence where Buttons crouched; sniffed, but stupidly failed to look up. Buttons looked down at him with contempt, as if saying to himself, 'Dogs only think in two dimensions, cats in three.' But the scary thing was when I shouted at the dog and it went through a hole in the fence into next door's garden. Buttons swivelled on the fence top, following every move. Then dropped down next door and began to *stalk* the great beast, a look of rapturous interest on his face.

I have known three kinds of cat. There are stupid cats, who are a worry. I had a neutered tom who would spend ages measuring a half-metre jump, eyeing and swaying backwards and forwards, then jump and miss his footing, and fall, clumsily and slink off shamefaced. Oh, yes, there are hopelessly stupid cats, though you still love them.

And then there are perfectly adequate cats, who follow a steady round of hunting, sunning, walking and sleeping, every minute of their day full, like a busy entirely contented little housewife. Like my Jemimah.

And then there are the highly intelligent cats, who seem to sense there is something more to life than being a cat; something that they have missed, and who go round endlessly wondering about it and looking for the missing clue. I grieve for them most of all. I sometimes have dreams that they are full-sized and able to talk, so I can explain the universe to them, at least as far as I have worked it out myself.

Such a cat was Buttons. Sometimes, when my daughters were laughing or fighting, he would give me an intense look as if to say, 'What the hell is going *on*?'

Still, he carried on his researches where he could. Like his experiments into the laws of gravity, when he would mount to a shelf or work-top, line up many small items at the edge, and knock them off one after the other, assessing their fall with quick keen flicks of the head, then giving me that hard enquiring stare.

Or his endless work with dripping taps, which would occupy him for an hour at a time, leaving him with his right paw and right ear soaked, but his mind none the wiser.

He never dozed, as most cats do. When he slept, he *slept* the sleep of utter exhaustion. But even then, his nose would wrinkle, his paw twitch, as if he had only transferred his endless researches to another sphere of being. He hated to be bored. When he was bored, he would give me that hard accusing stare, as if I had led him into a world that was a disappointment to him. I began to fear he might be one of those cats whom curiosity truly kills.

And then reports began coming back from the neighbours. (Always charming and pleasing ones, I might add.) One neighbour could not begin gardening without Buttons immediately appearing, and holding her arm still with an enquiring paw, while the turned earth was sniffed thoroughly and the end of her trowel marked with a rub of his jaw.

At another cottage, he would call at twelve every day, clean off the resident cat's saucer, and ascend the stairs to sleep an exhausted sleep for exactly an hour on the silk coverlet.

And then it was the turn of the church and the church hall. The latter had a steady round of meetings, none of which Buttons missed. He particularly liked the women's country dancing, lying like a pasha among the coats piled on the stage, watching the women prance and bounce with a head that was never still. He would have his share of milk and biscuits at half-time and ask to be let out exactly five minutes before the end.

More baffling was his love of meetings of the parochial church council, through which he would lie on the radiator, following every wild arm gesture while they debated with passion the replacing of broken slates. The caretaker was amazed at his timekeeping. He not only missed nothing, but was waiting there for the caretaker to unlock the door, five minutes before anything started. Then he took to attending church services, sitting on the steps to greet the congregation arriving, and again to greet them departing, and sitting in the back pew with the church-wardens in between. They tried keeping him out; but a cat is more than a match for any number of churchwardens when there are pews to run beneath, so in the end they let him be. And once he was missing three days, locked in the church, and the vicar's wife was astonished to find him sitting on the chancel steps watching the flickering flame of the sanctuary light with all the patient solemnity of a judge. We called him Holy Joe for a time after that, for as yet he had still not received his proper name.

That began with the television. We would come into a perfectly empty lounge to find a perfectly stupid programme running, that even the girls denied having switched on. Fearing a defective set or a poltergeist, we kept watch.

And one morning early, my wife was rewarded by seeing Buttons go over to the remote control, and trample all over it, where it lay on the coffee table. The set came on, hopped from channel to channel, went loud, soft, bright, dim, while Buttons trampled on and on, on the buttons, enjoying his feline son et lumière. Occasionally, though, he would desist; especially when *One Man and His Dog* came up, when he would go and lie on top of the set, and swat the tiny black dots that were the labouring sheepdogs, with an indolent and tolerant paw. We realised he must also be responsible for the unwanted video recordings of such wildly improbable shows as *Come Dancing* and Open University offerings on Victorian sewage-disposal . . . he was kept out of the lounge after that, except to perform his party-trick for visitors.

So you can see how he achieved what seemed the fullness of his fame, as far as the village was concerned. But the best was yet to come.

At the end of March, when the next cricket season began to stir into life, with the worthy freezing at the nets, and the unworthy discussing matches long ago in the pub, we began to hear some nasty rumours from Gunton. The old team had turned up nervously to practice at their new all-weather nets, only to find newcomers there before them. Smart young Londoners in white flannels. Smart young Londoners who had played for college or university, and who seemed to think that their jobs as computer programmers and systems analysts depended on getting a good batting average in the coming season, or taking a lot of wickets with their off-spinners. There was a bowler of leg breaks called C. M. A. Offaney, who had played for Cambridge three years after I had . . .

The old locals hadn't been chucked off the team; they simply hadn't been selected. On merit. They had been bowled out time and again; they had been hit for six all over the field. Kerry Turnbull had bought them drinks in the staff canteen afterwards, slapped them on the back and suggested they join his reserve side, which had not only been called into being, but had a full fixture list in a smaller league.

Being men of spirit, they had refused, and gone back to poaching, or taken up growing giant leeks instead. On the main team, only two locals remained.

'Turnbull's ambitious, reckon,' said Jack Strensham, our secretary. 'He's after promotion to the Doric League, seems likely.' It is possible to apply for promotion to the Dorics if you have an outstanding season with us.

'I'm not standing for this,' I said. 'I know a few good players myself who could do with a game. If they're going to play dirty . . .'

'Reckon the committee'll let you play two in any match,' said Jack. 'Guest players like. I'm not letting us be dragged down by Turnbull. And the lads won't like it.'

So that was how it went. The season started, I'd invite down a couple of useful guest stars for the weekend, we did well (we'd always done pretty well – always in the top three anyway) and soon we were second in the league.

To Gunton. With the match against Gunton only four weeks away.

*

15

Meanwhile, Buttons had discovered the cricket team, because our pitch was just the far side of the church. There, he found many new occupations. The ladies who did the match teas were bowled over in a trice, and many a slice of ham and saucer of milk was he slipped. But he was never a greedy cat. Not for food, anyway; more greedy for experience. Like walking up the steep tiled roof of the pavilion, to tap around the tiny stiff weather vane that is a miniature copy of the one at Lord's, while all the ladies called to him anxiously to come down. Or he would solemnly climb the huge oaks in pursuit of magpies that were not very impressed with either his size or his precarious footing, and met him in combat on the top twigs as equals, not giving an inch and putting him in real danger of losing an eye. Several times whole matches were stopped while he was coaxed down to safety, the away team often in the forefront of the rescue operation. (He actually gained us one draw that way, when we were hard-pressed.) And he made a habit of pursuing the one ball in a hundred heading towards the boundary that he fancied for some reason. Though he would leap over the stroke rather than intercept it, when he found out how hard the ball was on his nose. He was perhaps most help to us in his flirtations with the visiting deep fielders (as soon as he'd won the hearts of our deep fielders, he lost interest in them). He did give me a couple of unearned fours, as the fielder in question came out of a cat haunted daydream to find my drive streaking past him, to the frantic shouts of his team-mates.

And then, of course, he caught on to the idea of away matches. I don't know if young Scott Walker hadn't something to do with that; he always seemed to arrive in the car young Scott was travelling in, Scott by this time having won himself the high rank of assistant scorer. Then Buttons was able to practice his repertoire of skull-duggery in front of a brand-new audience. I worried at first that he might wander off at some away match and get lost. But he always seemed to know when it was time to go home, and I think Scott would have died rather than leave him behind.

*

Then even uglier rumours began to float round the league. Kerry Turnbull was a fast bowler, as I'd feared. And from the sound of it, that most unpleasant of creatures, a wildly inaccurate fast bowler. He didn't so much take wickets as put people in hospital. And laughed when he did so. He was a monster. *And* he had rows with the opposition umpires. His own umpire, of course, was too frightened to open his mouth . . .

The lads got windy, as the match against Gunton approached. There was muttered talk of body armour. I decided, as captain, that I'd better go and study this monster in action.

Our next match was against Sanditon Bottoms. Living up to their name, they were at present the new bottom-of-the-league club. Jack reckoned our team could cope with Sanditon without my help.

'You go and suss the bastard out, Skip.'

So I went back to Gunton in the gear of an off-duty farm labourer – stonewashed jeans, a very vulgar t-shirt saying 'Love Thy Neighbour – Frequently' which some enemy had once given me as a Christmas present, and a huge pair of shades. I bought a can of coke, leaned on a fence post and gave all my attention to the coming foe.

They were a nice little batting side. The young men knew how to use their feet, as they'd been taught at school. They knocked up 165 for five, and then declared. Kerry Turnbull didn't have to bat. At least he had the modesty to put himself in at number eight. He was obviously saving himself for his bowling.

I watched three of his opening overs, and knew I personally had nothing to worry about. He was fast – very fast – the fastest I'd seen since I played against Yorkshire for Cambridge. If someone had taken him in hand when he was young, he might have been a good bowler. But nobody had ever managed to take Kerry in hand in his life.

So he was untouched by human hand, as they say. His run was far too long, and would have soon sapped the energy of a lesser man. And he dropped his head before he released the ball. Some of his deliveries bounced three metres in front of him. One ball at least in every over was a wide, and very few got anywhere near the wicket. And he was careless with his feet. The opposition umpire no-balled him three times in quick succession, and there was a stand-up row in the middle of the pitch. There were a lot fewer no-balls after that; either Kerry had tidied up his act, or he'd terrified the umpire into submission.

And I did notice one thing. If he'd been particularly bad in an over, he slowed down for the last delivery, shortened his run, and put in a ball that was actually on the wicket. The two wickets he got were from those last balls. Otherwise, he just turned the batsmen into shaking jelly, so that they could be lapped up by the very moderate medium-paced seam bowler at the other end.

Oh, yes, I had it all nicely sussed-out, leaning against that post in the sun. I had my talk ready for the team on Tuesday night, on how the monster could be tamed.

When he really put a guy in hospital. I mean, the guy was led off by two fielders with his hands across his face and blood trickling through his hands . . . and the sports hack from *The Melbury Echo* was there, gobbling it all up. The headlines were going to be stupendous . . .

I walked out of the ground thoughtful and discouraged, after Gunton won. With a hundred runs to spare. As I left, I passed Harry Coe.

'Got the bastard sussed out then, Mr Moralee?' he muttered to me, hopefully and hoarsely.

So much for my farm hand disguise.

They were very quiet in the back of the car, all the way to Gunton. And there was a smell of whisky, always a bad sign. Worse, my two guest stars of the week just happened to be good seam bowlers who batted at nine and ten.

I decided our only chance was to win the toss and put Gunton in to bat. Give our lads time to sober up and get their nerve back.

I did win the toss, after Kerry had done his best to crush my hand in his monstrous paw. I hoped I'd still be able to hold my bat.

But my two new seam bowlers opened beautifully. They kept a perfect length, and were never off the stumps. They really kept Kerry's bright young men tied up. Kerry's blokes tapped and crawled; none of them got their eye in, or made more than ten. By the time Kerry came in, they were sixty-eight for six.

Meanwhile, Buttons, having made the rounds of my fielders and getting rather bored with lack of stimulus, decided to go in for his butterfly ballet all over the outfield. He never catches them, but he makes some beautiful leaps trying and gets much admired for it. He was rather taking attention off the game now. There was a gust of laughter and clapping from the watching ladies, as the umpire gave Kerry middle-and-leg. Kerry looked up with a glower. And saw that he had a rival for the crowd's attention.

'Get that bloody cat off the field!'

'S'our mascot,' said Jack resentfully, not quite sotto voce enough. 'We don't play without our mascot.'

Which brought Kerry across to shout at me. I dislike being shouted at. I was not one of his myriad underlings. As a solicitor, it is not part of my life style to be shouted at. But I told him, civilly enough, that it was impossible to catch Buttons in the open air. I knew. The whole team had once tried it.

Kerry told me I was a useless Pommie wimp. Set off in pursuit of Buttons himself, roaring his head off.

Buttons found avoiding him too boringly easy. He kept almost letting Kerry catch him, then streaking away through his outstretched hands. Finally, trying too hard, Kerry went arse over tip. There was a nervous titter of laughter from the crowd.

Instantly silenced, as Kerry looked at them. I've never seen anything so evil in this world as the way Kerry's glare silenced that titter.

The next minute, Kerry beckoned, and every member of his team, every spectating programmer and systems analyst, every staff wife, caterer, sales director and scorer were up on their feet in the pursuit of Buttons.

Buttons loved every minute. Never, in his wildest

dreams, had he ever expected so much fun. It lasted about twenty minutes, until Scott walked across, talking calmly to Buttons, who let himself be picked up and carried away to the car . . .

We returned, refreshed, to our game.

Kerry Turnbull was bowled by my seam bowler first ball. My seam bowler completed a hat trick and Gunton were all out for seventy-five, by far their lowest score of the season. Kerry spent the tea interval blaming it all on the cat and saying he was going to complain to the league. Our lot sat seething and their lot sat shaking. It was not a happy meal.

There was once a movie about a boxer, called *Raging Bull*. I forget who the boxer was, and which actor played him. But the title had stuck in my mind, and I could now only apply it to Kerry Turnbull, as he led his team out after tea. Genghis Khan, Martin Bormann, Jack the Ripper . . . the mind just boggled. You could have said there was blood on the sand, if there had been any sand.

All I could do was open the batting. In the changing room, my blokes were producing helmets with wire face-guards, and stuffing magazines round their ribs inside their shirts . . . I only got my fellow opener out on the pitch by agreeing to take first strike.

Kerry opened, his run-up longer than ever. The ball bounced about two metres in front of him, came lazily and unsubtly curving up, on the leg side, and I cracked it for six. I had never in all my life done anything so unwise, and so satisfying. Our lot, watching, went mad with joy. It didn't improve Kerry's temper, or his control. Nothing he bowled was near the wicket, one was no-balled, and I took twenty-two off that first over. I never felt so happy in my life. Until the umpire called 'over' and I realised I'd left Stan Fairclough to face the batting at the other end. With a helmet round his face he'd never worn before, and at least one thick magazine up his shirt.

With such distractions, it was amazing he lasted three balls. Then Nat Orme came out, and stopped halfway to borrow the damned helmet off him. Nat didn't last out that over either . . .

My team just washed away from under me, as if I was a boy standing on a sandcastle with the tide coming in. I tried desperately to keep the strike. But Billy Niles got run out when his helmet, too loose on his head, went twisted in mid-wicket. And Leslie Sears went back for his magazine when it fell out of his trousers, and got run out as well. And little Ned Foley had a tooth knocked out by Kerry Turnbull's second ball. To cut a wretched story short, my guest stars made five each, which did them credit, and we were all out for seventy and lost by five runs.

We left without shaking hands with the opposition; I think they felt it was more than their jobs were worth. The only cheerful one going home was Buttons.

Still, I was relieved it was over for the year, and we hadn't been as disgraced as some.

Until I remembered the Holdsby Cup.

Of course Gunton made it to the final. The trouble was, so did we. We were a good side that year, especially with my guest stars. I think the lads would've liked to lose in the semi-final to Mayston, but batsmen have a strange reluctance to throw their wickets away, when it comes to it. And the Mayston bowlers were just too hittable . . .

My team arrived for the final at Gunton in a fine state of nerves, and there were helmets all over the changing room, that they hadn't worn since the last time. And young Len Phillips suddenly passed out and collapsed snoring in the corner. Jack took one sniff at his breath, dug a near-empty hip flask out of the lad's blazer pocket, and pronounced an overkill of Dutch courage. That left us with ten men. If you didn't count little Scott Walker, which we didn't, though we might have given him a game against a kinder club, just for the experience. I'd only been able to raise eleven men in the first place by going round the team pleading. There was a rash of distant relatives' weddings that week, and wrists sprained harvesting . . .

21

'Oh, well,' I said 'ten men it'll have to be,' as I led them out.

Only to be stopped by a slight little man in blazer and flannels who said, 'I hear you're short of a man. D'you mind if I have a game?'

I thought I recognised him. 'It's Offaney, isn't it?' I asked stupidly. 'C. M. A. Offaney?'

He smiled, diffidently, and shook hands.

'You feeling suicidal or something?' I nodded to where Kerry was haranguing his troops by throwing cricket balls at them as hard as he could.

'I resigned this morning,' he said. 'I resigned the team and I resigned the firm. A bloke can take only so much from *that* creature.'

'Welcome aboard,' I said weakly.

Just then, Buttons came wandering out on to the pitch, where the other side were throwing the ball about.

Kerry Turnbull uttered a scream of rage, and threw the ball straight at Buttons. And for once his aim was perfect. If he'd hit Buttons on the head, he would undoubtedly have killed him. Instead, he hit him on the tail. Buttons has a slight kink there to this day.

But Buttons did not run away. He looked full in the face of his enemy; a long hard blank black stare, as if he would never forgive or forget him, as long as they both still lived. Then he turned his back in contempt and stalked off towards Gunton's electronic scoreboard, where young Scott was making himself comfortable with the others in the snug little cabin with its big open window.

I remember thinking at the time that Kerry Turnbull was making an awful lot of enemies very quickly . . .

Again I was lucky enough to win the toss; and again I put them in to bat. I had my two guest seam bowlers again, and they bowled well. But their novelty had worn off, and besides they weren't getting much of a curve on the ball, and Kerry's bright young men settled in as if their jobs depended on it. Which they probably did. If Kerry won the Holdsby Cup as well as the league, promotion to the Dorics was practically certain.

At lunch they were eighty for three. After lunch, Offaney emerged from the obscurity of the deep, where he had been lurking, bowled like the angel he was, and did quite a lot of damage. A hundred and ten for six . . .

And then Kerry walked in. I think he'd been flogging computers all the morning, at the big house, and he now saw Offaney for the first time.

'You little Pommie prick . . .'

Offaney grinned. His whole little face, which in repose was rather like a sad duck's, lit up. He tossed the ball up in the air, making it spin so much he looked like a conjurer.

'Give him middle-and-leg,' he said to the umpire.

That was an over I shall never forget, as long as I live. Offaney bowled so *slow*. The ball seemed to hang in the air, stationary, just beyond the reach of Kerry's bat. Then it dropped on a length, Kerry would swipe, and the ball simply wouldn't be there. Kerry lunged, swiped, fell in a heap, and watched the ball float over five times, just clear of the bails. Five times in succession it happened. It was like a bull fight; the raging bull and the vulnerable tempting matador.

The sixth ball, which hung the longest of all, seemed to just graze the bails. Nothing happened; our keeper caught the ball smack in his gloves.

And then a bail fell off.

Kerry went mad. Claimed the wind had blown the bail off.

Our umpire pointed out quite reasonably that there *wasn't* any wind. With great regret (and a very obvious gesture that none of the crowd missed) he pointed to the pavilion. And shouting that he was going to appeal to the M.C.C., Kerry had to walk. He undid his pads on the way to the pavilion, and left them lying on the pitch with his bat.

And Offaney just stood there grinning. I'm sure he'd planned every ball just the way it was. A great bowler; he did very well for Worcestershire the following year.

They folded up soon after. A hundred and fifteen all out.

*

We had a simple batting plan. I would open, and keep the strike when Kerry was bowling, and leave the others to face the medium-paced guy. I thus managed to persuade them to leave their bloody silly helmets in the changing rooms, and for a while it went quite well. Nat Orme made fifteen, and Billy Niles ten, and Stan Fairclough nine. And I had made Kerry pay bitterly for his loose ones, and the score stood at seventy for three at tea.

And then, just after tea, disaster struck. We tried to run two, and only managed one because their fielding was sharp, and Bill Butterfield was left facing Kerry's second ball.

I think every bit of hate that Kerry had been saving up all afternoon went into that ball, and it was accurate too. It came up off the shoulder of Bill's bat and knocked him unconscious. We carried him off and waited anxiously for the sound of ambulance sirens.

When Tiddser Braithwaite came in to bat, he was wearing one of those bloody helmets. And Kerry, slowing himself right down, got him first ball. And then he got Fatty Thompson, and walked round like he'd really done the hat trick, though Bill was not out, just coming round in hospital.

By the time I got back in control, we were eighty-five for eight, with not many overs left. And at ninety, Henry Brothers gave an easy catch. That just left Offaney. And Offaney would be the first to tell you he was the worst batsman in the league. Any league.

Still, he didn't wear a helmet . . .

I remember, while we were waiting for Offaney to come out, I looked round to make sure Buttons was all right. I couldn't see him anywhere at first. Then I noticed the waving plume of his tail in the big open window of the scorer's box under the red-glowing scoreboard. He'd obviously decided discretion was the better part of valour, and was sticking close to Scott.

And then Offaney came in, and I forgot Buttons, because my heart sank. Offaney didn't even ask for middle-and-leg. He just stood with a hopeless look on his face, holding his bat like it was a golf club. I just knew the medium-paced guy would get him first ball. In one over's time . . .

I had one over of a tiring Kerry to win the match. And the tiring Kerry was the cautious Kerry. He'd halved his run, and was starting to look where he was putting the ball. He was suddenly a danger. No more sixes.

The first ball kept low, and I could only block it.

I managed to turn the second to leg for four.

And the third.

And the fourth.

A hundred and two. Even two sixes couldn't win now.

As if pointing this out, Kerry bowled a loose one. I cracked it nearly as far as the main computer labs . . . so near and yet so far.

And Kerry's last ball was a full toss, and I sent it the same way.

Then I looked at Offaney and he looked back at me, without hope. His batting average for the season was well under one, and we both knew it.

So why was this clapping coming from the pavilion, and echoing around the ground? Why were my lot throwing their caps and copies of *The Independent* in the air? Why was Kerry looking like he could chew his way through his own turf, all the way back to Australia?

The scoreboard, the malevolent glowing red scoreboard said it all.

We seemed to have scored a hundred and sixteen for nine.

Somehow we'd won the Holdsby Cup.

Scott and Buttons came home with me in my car, because other people had gone off to celebrate alcoholically.

'I don't get it,' I said to Scott. 'I still don't get it. Give me that computer print-out.' I pulled up the car and studied it.

Suddenly I saw it.

Two extras in the last over.

'There *weren't* any extras in the last over . . .'

Scott giggled. A delicious sound from a delicious child.

'The scorer was watching the match so close – it was so tense.'

'Ye-es.'

'And, well, you know what Buttons is . . . you know what he does to the telly . . .'

'Ye-es.'

'He did it to the electronic scoreboard. Kept putting his paw on the 'extras' button. Nobody noticed. So you won.'

'But how could *nobody* notice . . .'

'Well, if they noticed, they didn't let on. He hasn't got any friends, you know – Turnbull. Even the scorer wanted him to lose.'

'You mean . . .'

'Buttons did it. And *I* reckon he did it on purpose. He kept waving his tail in the scorer's face, sort of blinding him.'

I can tell you a few more things. How Kerry Turnbull quite lost his taste for cricket, and went to set up another subsidiary company in America. How interest in cricket waned at Gunton Manor pretty quickly, and the village blokes got their club back, with all its smashing facilities, but are once again bottom of the league. But as for telling you what went on in the soul of Buttons, that's beyond me.

THE CREATURES IN THE HOUSE

Dawn broke over Southwold seafront.

The wind was blowing against the waves; white horses showed all the way to the horizon; smaller and smaller as if painted by some obsessional Dutch marine artist. On the horizon itself sat a steamship, square as a pan on a shelf, scarcely seeming to move.

Seafront deserted; beach-huts huddled empty in the rain. The only movement was a flaking flap of emulsion paint on the pier pavilion, tearing itself off in the wind.

Miss Forbes opened her eyes on her last day. Eyes grey and empty as the sea. She eased her body in the velvet reclining rocker in the bay window; luxurious once, now greased in black patches from the day and night shifting of her body. It was some years since she had been to bed. Beds meant sheets and sheets meant washing . . . She seldom left the bay window. She took her food off the front doorstep and straight on to the occasional table by her side. Once a week she took the remains to the dustbin. Otherwise there were just the trips to the toilet, and the weekly journey to the dripping tap in the kitchen for a pink-rosed ewerful of water.

She opened her eyes and looked at the sea and wondered what month it was. Her mind was clearer this morning than for a long time. The creature in the house had not fed on her mind for a week. There wasn't much of Miss Forbes' mind left to feed on. A few shreds of memory from the 'forties; a vague guilt at things not done. The creature itself was weakening. The creature knew a time would come soon when it had nothing to feed on at all. Then it would have to hibernate, like a dormouse or hedgehog. But first the creature must provide for its

27

future, while there was still time. There was something Miss Forbes had to do . . .

She rose shakily, after trying to straighten thick stockings of two different tones of grey. She went out into the hall, picked up the 1968 telephone directory and, her eyes squinting five centimetres off the page, looked up the solicitor's number.

She had difficulty making the solicitor's girl understand who she was; an old-standing client and a wealthy one. She mentioned the name of partner after partner . . . old Mr Sandbach had been dead twenty years . . . young Mr Sandbach retired last spring. Yes, she supposed Mr Mason would have to do . . . two o'clock?

Then she slowly climbed the stairs, slippered feet carving footprints in dust thicker than the worn staircarpet. In what had once been her bedroom she opened the mirrored wardrobe door, not even glancing at her reflection as it swung out at her.

She began to wash and comb and dress. With spells of sitting down to rest it took three hours. The creature had to lend her its own waning strength. Even then, Miss Forbes scarcely managed. The creature itself nearly despaired.

But between them, they coped. At half past one, Miss Forbes rang for a taxi, the ancient black phone trembling in her hand.

The taxi-driver watched her awestruck in his rear-view mirror. Two things clutched tightly in her gloved hand. A door key and a big lump of wallpaper with something scrawled on the back in a big childish hand. Like all his kind, he was good at reading things backwards in his mirror.

'I leave all my worldly possessions to my niece, Martha Vickers, providing she is unmarried and living alone at the time of my death. On condition that she agrees, and continues, to reside alone at 17 Marine Parade. Or if she is unable or unwilling to comply with my wishes, I leave all my possessions to my great-niece, Sarah Anne Walmsley . . .'

The taxi-man shuddered. *He'd* settle for a heart-attack at seventy . . .

'Suppose I spend all the money, sell the house and run?' asked Sally Walmsley. 'I mean what's to stop me?'

'Me, I'm afraid,' said Mr Mason, wiping the thick fur of dust off the hallstand of 17 Marine Parade, and settling his plump pinstriped bottom. 'We are the executors of your aunt's estate . . . we shall have to keep *some* kind of eye on you . . . it could prove unpleasant . . . I hope it won't come to that. Suppose you and I have dinner about once every six months and you tell me what you've been up to . . .' He smiled tentatively, sympathetically. He liked this tall, thin girl with green eyes and long black hair. 'Of course, you could contest the will. It wouldn't stand up in court a moment. I couldn't *swear* your aunt was in her right mind the morning she made it. Not of sound testamentary capacity, as we say. But if you break the will, it would have to be shared with all your female aunts and cousins – married and unmarried. You'd get about ten thousand each – not a lot.'

'*Stuff them*,' said Sally Walmsley. 'I'll keep what I've got.' She suddenly felt immensely weary. The last six months had happened so fast. Deciding to walk out of art school. Walking out of art school. Trailing London looking for work. Getting a break as assistant art director of *New Woman*. And then lovely Tony Harrison of Production going back to his fat, frigid suburban cow of a wife. And then this . . .

'I must be off,' said Mr Mason, getting off the hallstand and surveying his bottom for dust in the spotted stained mirror. But he lingered in the door, interminably, as if guilty about leaving her. 'It was a strange business . . . I've dealt with a lot of old ladies, but your aunt . . . she looked . . . faded. Not potty, just *faded*. I kept on having to shout at her to bring her back to herself.

'The milkman found her, you know. When the third bottle of milk piled up on her doorstep. He always had the rule to let three bottles pile up. Old ladies can be funny. She might have gone away. But there she was, sitting in the bedroom bay window, grey as dust.

'He seems to have been her only human contact – money and scribbled notes pushed into the milk bottles. She lived on what he brought – bread, butter, eggs, yoghurt, cheese, orange juice. She seems to have never tried to cook – drank the eggs raw after cracking them into a cup.

'But she didn't die of malnutrition . . . the coroner said it was a viable diet, though not a desirable one. Didn't die of hypothermia, either. It was a cold week in March, but the gas fire was full on, and the room was like an oven . . .' He paused, as if an unpleasant memory had struck him. 'In fact, the coroner couldn't find any cause of death at all. He said she just seemed to have faded away . . . put it down to good old natural causes. Well, I must be off. If there's any way I can help . . .'

Sally nearly said, 'Please don't go.' But that would have been silly. So she smiled politely while he smiled too, bobbed his head and left.

Sally didn't like that at all. She listened to the silence in the house, and her skin crawled.

A primitive man, a bushman or aborigine, would have recognised that crawling of the skin. Would have left the spot immediately. Or if the place had been important to him, a cave or spring of water, he would have returned with other primitive men and performed certain rituals. And then the creature would have left.

But Sally simply told herself not to be a silly fool, and forced herself to explore.

The library was books from floor to ceiling. Avant-garde – fifty years ago. Marie Stopes, Havelock Ellis, the early Agatha Christie, Shaw and Wells. Aunt Maude had been a great reader, a Girton girl, a bluestocking. So what had she read the last ten years? For the fur of dust lay over the books as it lay over everything else. And there wasn't a magazine or paper in the house. So what had she *done* with herself, never going out, doing all her business by post, never putting stamps on her letters till the bank manager began sending her books of stamps of his own volition. Even the occasional plumber or meter-reader had never seen her; only a phone message and the front door open, with scrawled instructions pinned to it . . .

Aunt Maude might as well have been an enclosed nun . . .

But the house with its wood-planked walls, its red-tiled roof, its white gothic pinnacles, balconies and many bay windows was not in bad shape; nowhere near falling down. Nothing fresh paint wouldn't cure. And there was plenty of money. And the furniture was fabulously Victorian. Viennese wallclocks, fit only for the junkshop twenty years ago, would fetch hundreds now, once their glass cases were cleared of cobwebs, and their brass pendulums of verdigris. And the dining-room furniture was Sheraton; genuine, eighteenth-century Sheraton. Oh, she could make it such a place . . . where everybody would bother to come, even from London. Everybody liked a weekend by the sea. Even Tony Harrison . . . she thrust the thought down savagely. But what a challenge, bringing the place back to life.

So why did she feel like crying? Was it just the dusk of a November afternoon; the rain-runnelled dirt on the windows?

She reached the top of the house; a boxroom under the roof with a sloping ceiling. A yellow stained-glass window at one end that made it look as if the sun was always shining outside; the massed brick of the chimney-stacks at the other. A long narrow tall room; a wrong room that made her want to slam the door and run away. Instead, she made herself stand and *analyse* her feelings. Simple, really; the stained glass was alienating; the shape of the room was uncomfortable, making you strain upwards and giving you a humiliating crick in the neck. Simple, really, when you had art-school training, an awareness of the psychology of shape and colour.

She was still glad to shut the door, go downstairs to the kitchen with its dripping tap, and make herself a cup of tea. She left all the rings of the gas stove burning. *And* the oven. Soon the place was as warm as a greenhouse. . .

*

In the darkest corner of the narrow boxroom, furthest from the stained-glass window where the sun always seemed to shine, up near the grey-grimed ceiling, the creature stirred in its sleep. It was not the fiercest or strongest of its kind; not quite purely spirit, or rather decayed from pure spirit. It could pass through the wood and glass of doors and windows easily, but it had difficulty with brick and stonework. That was why it had installed Miss Forbes in the bay window; so it could feed on her quickly, when it returned hungry from its long journeys. It fed on humankind, but not all humankind. It found workmen in the house quite unbearable; like a herd of trampling, whistling, swearing elephants. Happy families were worse, especially when the children were noisy. It only liked women, yet would have found a brisk WI meeting an unbearable hell. It fed on women alone; women in despair. It crept subtly into their minds, when they slept or tossed and worried in the middle of the night, peeling back the protective shell of their minds that they didn't even know they had; rather as a squirrel cracks a nut, or a thrush a snail-shell; patient, not hurryng, delicate, persistent . . .

Like all wise parasites it did not kill its hosts. Miss Forbes had lasted it forty years; Miss Forbes' great-aunt had lasted nearer sixty.

Now it was awake, and hungry.

Sally hugged her third mug of tea between her hands and stared out of the kitchen window, at the long dead grass and scattered dustbins of the November garden. The garden wall was fifty metres away, sooty brick. There was nothing else to see. She had the conviction that her new life had stopped; that her clockwork was running down. I could stand here forever, she thought in a panic. I must go upstairs and make up a bed; there was plenty of embroidered lavendered Edwardian linen in the drawers. But she hadn't the energy.

I could go out and spend the night in an hotel. But which hotels would be open, in Southwold in November?

She knew there was a phone, but British Telecom had cut it off.

Just then, something appeared suddenly on top of the sooty wall, making her jump. One moment it wasn't there; next moment it was.

A grey cat. A tomcat, from the huge size of its head and thickness of shoulder.

It glanced this way and that; then lowered its forefeet delicately down the vertical brick of the wall, leapt and vanished into the long grass.

She waited; it reappeared, moving through the long grass with a stalking lope so like a lion's and so unlike a cat indoors. It went from dustbin to dustbin, sniffing inside each in turn, without hope and without success. She somehow knew it did the same thing every day, at the same time. It had worn tracks through the grass.

Hard luck, she thought, as the cat found nothing. Then spitefully, Sucker! She hated the cat, because its search for food was so like her own search for happiness.

The cat sniffed inside the last bin unavailingly, and was about to depart, empty-handed.

Welcome to the club, thought Sally bitterly.

It was then that the hailstorm came; out of nowhere, huge hailstones, slashing, hurting. The tomcat turned, startled, head and paw upraised, snarling as if the hailstorm was an enemy of its own kind, as if to defend itself against this final harshness of life.

Sally felt a tiny surge of sympathy.

It was almost as if the cat sensed it. It certainly turned towards the kitchen window and saw her for the first time. And immediately ran towards her, and leapt on to the lid of a bin directly under the window, hailstones belting small craters in its fur, and its mouth open; red tongue and white teeth exposed in a silent miaow that was half defiance and half appeal.

You can't let this happen to me.

It made her feel like God; the God she had often screamed and wept and appealed to; and never had an answer.

I am *kinder* than God, she thought in sad triumph, and ran to open the kitchen door.

The cat streaked in, and, finding a dry shelter, suddenly remembered its dignity. It shook itself violently, then shook the wetness off each paw in turn, as a kind of symbol of disgust with the weather outside, then began to vigorously belabour its shoulder with a long pink tongue.

But not for long. Its nose began to twitch; began to twitch quite monstrously. It turned its head, following the twitch, and leapt gently on to the kitchen table, where a packet lay, wrapped in paper.

A pound of mince, bought in town earlier, and forgotten. Sally sat down, amused, and watched. All right, she thought, if you can get it, you can have it.

The cat tapped and turned the parcel, as if it were a living mouse. Seemed to sit and think for a moment, then got its nose under the packet and, with vigorous shoves propelled it to the edge of the table, and sent it thumping on to the stone floor.

It was enough to burst the paper the butcher had put round it. The mince splattered across the stone flags with all the gory drama of a successful hunt. The cat leapt down and ate steadily, pausing only to give Sally the occasional dark suspicious stare, and growling under its breath.

OK, thought Sally. You win. I'd never have got round to cooking it tonight, and there isn't a fridge . . .

The cat extracted and hunted down the last red crumb, and then began exploring the kitchen; pacing along the work-tops, prying open the darkness of the cupboards with an urgent paw.

There was an arrogance about him, a sense of taking possession, that could make her think of only one thing to call him.

When he finally sat down, to wash and survey her with blank dark eyes, she called softly, 'Boss? Boss?'

He gave a short and savage purr and leapt straight on to her knee, trampling her about with agonising sharp claws, before finally settling in her lap, facing outwards, front claws clenched in her trousered knees. He was big, but painfully thin. His haunches felt like bone knives under his matted fur. The fat days must be in the summer, she thought sleepily, with full dustbins behind every hotel. What do they do in November?

He should have been an agony; but strangely he was a comfort. The gas stove had made the room deliciously warm. His purring filled her ears.

They slept, twisted together like symbiotic plants, in a cocoon of contentment.

The creature sensed Sally's sleep. It drifted out of the boxroom and down the intricately carved staircase, like a darkening of the shadows; a dimming of the faint beams that crept through the filthy net curtains from a distant street-lamp.

Boss did not sense it until it entered the kitchen. A she-cat would have sensed it earlier. But Boss saw it, as Sally would never see it. His claws tightened in Sally's knee; he rose up and arched his back and spat, ears laid back against his skull. Sally whimpered in her sleep, trying to soothe him with a drowsy hand. But she didn't waken . . .

Cat and creature faced each other. Boss felt no fear, as a human might. Only hate at an intruder, alien, enemy.

And the creature felt Boss's hate. Rather as a human might feel a small stone that has worked its way inside a shoe. Not quite painful; not enough to stop for, but a distraction.

The creature could not harm Boss; their beings had nothing in common. But it could press on his being; press abominably.

It pressed.

Boss leapt off Sally's knee. If a door had been open, or a window, Boss would have fled. But no door or window was open. He ran frantically here and there, trying to escape the black pressure, and finally ended up crouched in the corner under the sink, protected on three sides by brickwork, but silenced at last.

Now the creature turned its attention to Sally, probing at the first layer of her mind.

Boss, released, spat and swore terribly.

It was as if, for the creature, the stone in the shoe had turned over, exposing a new sharp edge.

The creature, exploding in rage, pressed too hard on the outer layer of Sally's mind.

Sally's dream turned to nightmare, a nightmare of a horrible female thing with wrinkled dugs and lice in her long grey hair. Sally woke, sweating.

The creature was no longer there.

Sally gazed woozy-eyed at Boss, who emerged from under the sink, shook himself, and immediately asked to be let out the kitchen door. Very insistently. Clawing at the woodwork.

Sally's hand was on the handle, when a thought struck her. If she let the cat out, she would be *alone*.

The thought was unbearable.

She looked at Boss.

'Hard luck, mate,' she said. 'You asked to be let in. You've had your supper. Now bloody earn it!'

As if he sensed what she meant, Boss gave up his attempts on the door. Sally made some tea; and conscience-stricken, gave Boss the cream off the milk. She looked at her watch. Midnight.

They settled down again.

Three more times that night the creature tried. Three times with the same result. It grew ever more frantic, clumsy. Three times Sally had nightmares and woke sweating, and made tea.

Boss, on the other hand, was starting to get used to things. The last time, he did not even stir from Sally's knee. Just lay tensely and spat. The black weight of the creature seemed less when he was near the human.

After three a.m. cat and girl slept undisturbed. While the creature roamed the stairs and corridors, demented. Perhaps it was beginning to realise that one day, like Miss Forbes and Miss Forbes's great-aunt, it too, might simply cease to exist; like the corpse of a hedgehog, by a country road, it might slowly blow away into particles of dust.

*

A weak morning sunlight cheered the dead grass of the garden. Sally opened a tin of corned beef and gave Boss his breakfast. He wolfed the lot, and then asked again to be let out, with renewed insistence.

Freedom was freedom, thought Sally sadly. Besides, if he didn't go soon there was liable to be a nasty accident. She watched him go through the grass, and gain the top of the wall with a magnificent leap.

Then he vanished, leaving the world totally empty.

She spent four cups of coffee gathering her wits; then opened her suitcase, washed at the kitchen sink, and set out to face the world.

It wasn't bad. The sky was pale blue, every wave was twinkling like diamonds as it broke on the beach, and her brave new orange Mini stood parked twenty metres down the road.

But it was Boss she watched for; in the tangled front garden, on the immaculate lawn of the house next door.

Then she looked back at number 17, nervously. It looked all right, from here . . .

'Good morning!' The voice made her jump.

The owner of number 16 was straightening up from behind his well-mended fence, a handful of dead brown foliage in one hand.

He was everything she disliked in a man. About thirty. Friendly smile, naive blue eyes, check shirt, folk-weave tie. He offered a loamy paw, having wiped it on the seat of his gardening trousers.

'Just moved in then? My name's Mike Taverner. Dwell here with my mama . . .'

Half an hour later she broke away, her head spinning with a muddling survey of all the best shops in town and what they were best for. The fact that Mr Taverner was an accountant and therefore worked gentleman's hours. That he was quite handy round the house and that if anything he could do . . . But it was his subtly pitying look that was worst.

Stuff him! If *he* thought that *she* was going to ask *him* round for coffee . . .

She spent the day using Miss Forbes' money. A huge

hand-torch for some reason; a new transistor radio, satisfyingly loud; a check tablecloth; three new dresses, the most with-it that Southwold could offer. She'd ordered a new gas stove, and gained the promise that British Telecom would reconnect tomorrow . . .

She still had to go home in the end.

She put her new possessions on the kitchen table, all in a mass, and they just seemed to shrink to the size of Dinky Toys. The silence of the house pressed on her skin like a cold moist blanket.

But she was firm. Went upstairs and made the bed, in the front bedroom with the bay window. Then sat over her plate of bacon and eggs till it congealed solid. The sounds that came out of the transistor radio seemed like alien code messages from Mars.

She went to bed at midnight, clutching the tranny under one arm, and fags, matches, torch, magazines with the other.

But before she went, she left the kitchen window open four inches. And a fresh plate of mince on the sill. It was like a hundred-to-one bet on the Grand National . . .

Boss left the house determined never to return, and picked up the devious trail through alley and garden, backyard and beach-shelter that marked the edge of his territory, smelling his old trademarks and renewing them vigorously. He stalked and killed a hungry sparrow in one alley; found some cinder-embedded bacon rind in another, but that was all. He was soon hungry again.

By the time dusk was falling, and he rendezvoused at the derelict fishermen's hut with his females, he was very hungry indeed. The memory of the black terror had faded; the memory of the raw mince grew stronger.

He sniffed noses and backsides with one of his females in particular, a big scrawny tortoiseshell with hollow flanks and bulging belly. But he could not settle. The memory of the mince grew to a mountain in his mind; a lovely blood-oozing salty mountain.

Around midnight, he got up and stretched, and headed out again along his well-beaten track.

Ten metres behind, weak and limping, the tortoiseshell followed. She followed him further than she had ever ventured before; but she was far more hungry than him; her plight far more desperate. And she had smelt the rich raw meat on his breath . . .

The creature felt them enter the house; now there were two sharp stones in its shoe.

It had been doing well before they came. Sally had taken two Mogadon, and lay sleeping on her back, mouth open and snoring, a perfect prey. The creature was feeding gently on the first layer of her mind; lush memories of warmth and childhood, laughter and toys. First food in six months.

Uneasy, suddenly it fed harder; too hard. Sally moaned and swam up slowly from her drugged sleep; sat up and knew with terror that something precious had been stolen from her; was missing, gone for ever.

The creature did not let go of her, hung on with all its strength; it was so near to having her completely.

Sally felt as cold as death under the heaped blankets; the sheets were like clammy winding-sheets, strangling, smothering. She fought her way out of them and reeled about the room, seeking blindly for the door in the dark. Warm, she must get warm or . . .

The kitchen . . . gas stove . . . warm. Desperately she searched the walls for the door, in the utter dark. Curtains, windows, pictures swinging and falling under her grasping hands. She was crying, screaming . . . Was there no door to this black room?

Then the blessed roundness of the door handle, that would not turn under her cold-sweating palm, until she folded a piece of her nightdress over it. And then she was going downstairs, half-running, half-falling, bumping down the last few steps on her bottom, in the dim light of the street-lamp through the grimy curtains . . .

The whole place rocked still in nightmare, because the creature still clung to her mind . . .

Twice she passed the kitchen door, and then she found it and broke through, and banged the light on.

Check tablecloth; suitcase; tweed coat. Sally's eyes

clutched them, like a drowning man clutches straws. The creature felt her starting to get away; struggling back to the real world outside.

But much worse, the creature felt two pairs of eyes glaring; glaring hate. The tomcat was crouched on the old wooden draining-board, back arched. But the tom was not the worst. The she-cat lay curled on a pathetic heap of old rags and torn-up newspaper under the sink. And her hatred was utterly immovable and there were five more small sharp stones now in the creature's shoe. A mild squeaking came from within the she-cat's protective legs. Little scraps of blind fur, writhing . . .

Sally's mind gave a tremendous heave and the creature's hold broke. The creature could not stand the she-cat's eyes, alien, blank, utterly rejecting.

It fled back up the stairs, right to the boxroom, and coiled itself in the dark corner, between a high shelf and the blackened ceiling.

It knew, as it lapsed into chaos, that there was one room in its house where it dared never go again.

Back in the kitchen, Sally closed the door and then the window, and lit all the rings of the gas stove. The tom cat shook itself and rubbed against her legs, wanting milk.

'Kittens,' said Sally, 'kittens. Oh you *poor* thing.'

But at that moment there was nothing in the world she wanted more than kittens. She put on a saucepan, and filled it to the brim with milk.

She felt Boss stir off her knee towards dawn. She opened her eyes, and saw him on the windowsill, asking to go out.

'All right,' she said reluctantly. She opened the window. She knew now that he would come back. Besides, the purring heap of cat and kittens, now installed on a pile of old curtains in an armchair, showed no sign of wanting to move. She would not be alone . . .

She left the window open. It was not a very cold night, and the room was now too hot if anything, from the gas stove.

She was wakened at eight, by Boss's pounding savage claws on her lap. He made loud demands for breakfast.

And he was not alone. There was a black-and-white female sitting washing itself on the corner of the table; and a white-and-ginger female was curled up with the mother and kittens, busy washing all and sundry. The aunties had arrived.

'Brought the whole family, have you?' she asked Boss sourly. 'Sure there aren't a few grandmas you forgot?'

He gave a particularly savage purr, and dug his claws deeper into her legs.

'OK,' she said. 'How would Tyne-Brand meat loaf do? With pilchards for starters?'

By the time they had finished, the larder was bare. They washed, and Sally ate toast and watched them washing. She thought, I'm bonkers. Only old maids have cats like this. People will think I'm mad. The four cats regarded her with blandly friendly eyes. Somehow it gave her courage to remember the nightmare upstairs . . .

Then the cats rose, one by one. Nudged and nosed each other, stretched, began to mill around.

It reminded her of something she'd once seen; on telly somewhere.

Lionesses, setting off to hunt. That was it. Lionesses setting off to hunt.

But for God's sake, they'd *had* their breakfast . . .

Boss went to the door and miaowed. Not the kitchen door; the door that led to the nightmare staircase. Mother joined him. And Ginger. And the black-and-white cat she'd christened Chequers.

When she did not open the door, they all turned and stared at her. Friendly; but expectant. Compelling.

My God, she thought. They're going hunting whatever is upstairs. And inviting me to join in . . .

They were the only friends she had. She went; but she picked up Boss before she opened the door. He didn't seem to mind; he settled himself comfortably in her arms, pricking his ears and looking ahead. His body was vibrating. Purr or growl deep in his throat. She could not tell.

The she-cats padded foward, looked at the doors of the

downstairs rooms, then leapt up the stairs. They nosed into everything, talking to each other in their prooky spooky language. They moved as if they were tied to each other and to her with invisible strands of elastic; passing each other, weaving from side to side like a cat's cradle, but never getting too far ahead, or too far apart.

They went from upstairs room to upstairs room, politely standing aside as she opened each door. Leaping on to dust-sheeted beds, sniffing in long-empty chamber pots.

Each of the rooms was empty; dreary, dusty, but totally empty. Sally wasn't afraid. If anything, little tingling excitements ran through her.

The cats turned to the staircase that led to the boxroom in the roof. They were closer together now, their chirrups louder, more urgent.

They went straight to the door of the narrow room, with the yellow stained-glass window that was always sunshine.

Waited. Braced. Ears back close to the skull.

Sally took a deep breath and flung open the door.

Immediately the cold came, the clammy winding-sheet cold of the night before. The corridor, the stairs twisted and fell together like collapsing stage scenery.

She would have run; but Boss's claws, deep and sharp in her arm, were realler than the cold and the twisting – like an anchor in a storm. She stood. So did the cats, though they crouched close to the floor, huddled together.

Slowly, the cold and twisting faded.

The cats rose and shook themselves, as after a shower of rain, and stalked one by one into the boxroom.

Trembling, Sally followed.

Again the sick cold and twisting came. But it was weaker. Even Sally could tell that. And it didn't last so long.

The cats were all staring at the ceiling at the far end; at a dark grey space between the heavy brickwork of two chimneys; between the ceiling and a high wooden shelf.

Sally stared too. But all she could see was a mass of cobwebs; black rope-like strands blowing in some draught that came through the slates of the roof.

But she knew her enemy, the enemy who had stolen from her, was there. And for the first time, because the enemy was now so small, no longer filling the house, she could feel anger, red healthy anger.

She looked round for a weapon. There was an old short-bristled broom leaning against the wall. She put down Boss and picked it up, and slashed savagely at the swaying cobwebs, until she had pulled every one of them down.

They clung to the broomhead.

But they were only cobwebs.

Boss gave a long chirrup. Cheerful, pleased, but summoning. Slowly, in obedience, the three she-cats began to back out of the door, never taking their green eyes from the space up near the ceiling.

Sally came last, and closed the door.

They retired back to the kittens, in good order.

Back in the boxroom, the creature was absolutely still. It had learnt the bitter limitations of its strength. It had reached the very frontier of its existence.

It grew wise.

Back in the kitchen, there came a knock on the door.

It was Mr Taverner. Was she all right? He thought he had heard screams in the night . . .

'It was only Jack the Ripper,' said Sally with a flare of newfound spirit. 'You're too late – he murdered me.'

He had the grace to look woebegone. He had quite a nice lopsided smile, when he was woebegone. So she offered him a cup of coffee.

He sat down and the she-cats climbed all over him, sniffing in his ears with spiteful humour. Standing on his shoulders with their front paws on top of his head . . . He suffered politely, with his lopsided grin. 'Have they moved in on you? Once you feed them, they'll never go away . . . they're a menace round Southwold, especially in the winter. I could call the RSPCA for you . . .?'

'They are *my* cats. I *like* cats.'

He gave her a funny look. 'They'll cost you a bomb to feed . . .'

'I know how much cats cost to feed. And don't think I can't afford to keep a hundred cats if I want to.'

Again he had the grace to shut up.

Things went better for Sally after that. Mike Taverner called in quite often, and even asked her to have dinner with his mother. Mrs Taverner proved not to be an aged burden, but a smart fifty-year-old who ran a dress-shop, didn't discuss hysterectomies, and watched her son's social antics with a wry long-suffering smile.

The kittens grew; the house filled with whistling workmen; the Gas Board came finally to install the new cooker.

And Sally took to sleeping on the couch of a little breakfast room just off the kitchen; where she could get a glimpse of sea in the mornings, and the cats came and went through the serving-hatch.

She slept well, usually with cats coming and going off her feet all night. Sometimes they called sharply to each other, and there was a scurrying of paws, and she would waken sweating. That noise meant the creature from the boxroom was on the prowl.

But it never tried anything, not with the cats around.

And every day, Sally and the cats did their daily patrol into enemy territory. What Sally came to think of, with a nervous giggle, as the bearding of the boxroom.

But the creature never reacted. The patrols became almost a bore, and pairs of cats could be heard chasing each other up and down the first flight of stairs, on their own.

What a crazy life, Sally thought. If Mike Taverner *dreamt* what was going on, what would he say? Once, she even took him on a tour of the house, to admire the new decorations. Took him right into the boxroom. All the cats came too.

The creature suffered a good deal from Mike's elephantine soul and great booming male voice . . .

But the boundary between victory and defeat is narrow; and usually composed of complacency.

The last night started so happily. Mike was coming to dinner; well, he was better than *nothing*. Sally, in her newest dress and butcher's apron, was putting the finishing touches to a sherry trifle. A large Scotch sirloin steak lay wrapped in a bloody package on the fridge, handy for the gas cooker.

Sally had just nipped into the breakfast room to lay the table when she heard a rustling noise in the kitchen . . .

She rushed back in time to see Boss nosing at the bloody packet.

She should have picked him up firmly; but chose to shoo him away with a wild wave of her arms. Boss, panicking, made an enormous leap for the window. The sherry trifle, propelled by all the strength of his back legs, catapulted across the room and self-destructed on the tiled floor in a mess of cream and glass shards a metre wide.

Sally went berserk. Threw Boss out of the back door; threw Chequers after him, and slammed the window in Mother's face, just as Mother was coming in.

That only left the kittens, eyes scarcely open, crawling and squeaking in their basket. She would have some peace for once, to get ready.

Maybe Mike was right. Too many cats. Only potty old maids had so many cats. RSPCA . . . good homes.

She never noticed that the kittens had ceased to crawl and squeak and maul each other. That they grew silent and huddled together in one corner of their basket, each trying desperately to get into the middle of the heap of warm furry bodies . . .

She scraped and wiped up the trifle. Made Mike an Instant Whip instead. In a flavour she knew he didn't like. Well, he could lump it. Sitting round her kitchen all day, waiting to have his face fed. Fancy living with *that* face for forty years . . . growing bald, scratching under the armpits of his checked shirt like an ape. He'd only become interested in her seriously when he heard about her money . . . Stuff him. Better to live alone . . .

Mike was unfortunate enough to ring up at that point. He was bringing wine. Would Chateauneuf-du-Pape do? How smug he sounded; how sure he had her in his grasp.

He made one of his clumsy teasing jokes. She chose to take it the wrong way. Her voice grew sharp. He whinged self-righteously in protest. Sally told him what she *really* thought of him. He rang off in high dudgeon, implying he would never bother her again.

Good. Good riddance to bad rubbish. Much better living on her own in her beautiful house, without a great clumsy corny man in it. . .

But his rudeness had given her a headache. Might as well take a Mogadon and lie down. She suddenly felt cold and really tired . . . sleep it off.

Boss was crazy for the sirloin; Mother was very worked-up about her kittens; and the window-catch was old and rusted. Five minutes' work had the window open. Mother made straight for her kittens and Boss made straight for the meat. Three heaves and he had the packet open, and the kitchen filled with the rich smell of blood. Ginger and Chequers appeared out of nowhere and Mother, satisfied her brood was safe, rapidly joined them in a baleful circle round the fridge.

They were not aware of the creature, in their excitement. It was in the breakfast room with Sally, behind a closed door and feeding quietly.

But Boss was infuriatedly aware of the other cats, as they stretched up the face of the fridge, trying to claw his prize out of his mouth. He sensed he would have no peace to enjoy a morsel. So, arching his neck magnificently to hold the steak clear of the floor, he leapt down, then up to the windowsill and out into the night.

Unfortunately, it was one of those damp warm nights that accent every odour; and the faintest of breezes was blowing from the north towards the town centre of Southwold. Several hungry noses lifted to the fascinating new scent.

Within a minute, Boss knew he was no longer alone. Frantically he turned and twisted through his well-known alleyways. But others knew them just as well, and the scent was as great a beacon as the circling beams of Southwold's lighthouse. Even the well-fed domestic tabbies, merely out for an airing, caught it. As for the hungry desperate ones . . .

Boss was no fool. He doubled for home. Came through the window like a rocket, leaving a rich red trail on the yellowed white paintwork, and regained the fridge. Another minute, and there were ten strange cats in the room. Two minutes and there were twenty.

Boss leapt for the high shelving in desperate evasion. A whole shelf of pots and pans came down together. The noise beggared description, and there were more cats coming in all the time.

Next door the creature, startled, slipped clumsily in its feeding. Sally came screaming up out of nightmare and ran for the warmth of her kitchen, the creature still entangled in her mind.

To the creature, the kitchenful of cats was like rolling in broken glass. Silently, it fled to the high shelf in the boxroom.

It was unfortunate for the creature that Boss had very much the same thought. The hall door was ajar. He was through it in a flash and up the stairs, the whole frantic starving mob in pursuit.

Back in the near-empty kitchen, there came a thunderous knocking on the door. It burst open to reveal Mr Taverner in a not-very-becoming plum-coloured smoking jacket. He flung his arms round Sally, demanding wildly to know what the matter was.

Sally could only point mutely upstairs.

By the time they got there, Boss, with slashing claws and hideous growls that filtered past the sirloin steak, was making his last stand in the open boxroom door.

And, confused and bewildered by so many enemies, weak from hunger and shattered by frustration, the creature was cowering up on its shelf, trying to get out into the open air through the thick brickwork of the chimneys. But it was old, old . . .

Boss, turning in desperation from the many claws dabbing at his steak, saw the same high shelf and leapt.

Thirty pairs of ravening cat-eyes followed him.

The creature knew, for the first time in its ancient existence, how it felt to be prey . . .

It lost all desire to exist.

Nobody heard the slight popping noise, because of the din. But suddenly there was a vile smell, a rubbish-tip, graveyard, green-water smell.

And the house was empty of anything but dust and cobwebs, woodlice and woodworm. Empty for ever.

THE NAMING OF CATS

The shopkeepers just called him Old Blackie. Though he was only four, the set solidity of his bulk, the thickness of his fur against the night cold on windy corners, the scars on his forehead and ears which never quite healed, made him look older than he was.

He was popular; the butcher's assistant saved scraps for him which she dropped in the sawdust surreptitiously when the butcher wasn't looking. He must have eaten a lot of sawdust in his time. He was allowed to sleep in the midday sun streaming over the shoddy brass objects in the post office window. In the evenings, he huddled on the assistant's small stool behind the counter in the off licence, just above the gusts of the fan-heater which stirred his fur into constant motion. Only when the shops closed was he on his own in a bleak world of brick corners and drifting frozen snow.

Had he been able to give a name to himself, he would probably have called himself the Black Cat. He was very aware of being a cat, totally interested in catness; the merest sight of another pair of feline ears, pricking over a hedge, made him quiver with intentness, lash his tail, and flick his head from side to side with rapid movements, to get a better view. And he must have been convinced of his blackness, since his pink tongue cleansed it so often and so lovingly. He was clean, for a tom, fussy with himself. He never sprayed indoors; he had long ago learnt it cut off his supplies of food and warmth.

He was deeply affectionate, but had to live on the crumbs of caresses from busy shoppers he accosted boldly and politely, with an upward butt of his head to the descending hand. Deep inside himself, he felt it was not enough; he felt there was something he was missing, though he did not know what it was.

Still, he kept permanently on the lookout for it, for anything new.

Which was how he found the student hostel.

Late one night, he encountered a drunk. He had mixed feelings about drunks. They were a source of interest, when everyone else was safely locked up in their houses for the night. Sometimes they would fall down and have great grunting difficulty getting up again, which would while away a whole half-hour. Sometimes they would relieve themselves behind the overgrown privet of neglected front gardens, with the sound of a rushing waterfall. Sometimes they would subside with their backs against a garden wall and tell Blackie all their sins with maudlin guilt.

'By, Aah've been a bad beggar in me time, Blackie! Aah've committed many a sin, a mortal sin.' Then they would weep and feel better, while the cat sat as silent and objective as a Roman Catholic priest in the confessional.

Sometimes they gave him food; the remains of a bag of crisps, that made him shake his head and shudder at the strength of the salt; or a well-chewed quarter of pork pie, nearly all crust. But it was all grist to his mill; even in the dark he located and mouthed-up every last crumb.

But this particular night, this particular drunk was different. He was young, good-looking in a thin duffle-coated way, though his tangled hair and beard seldom saw a comb, unless it was his long thin fingers that combed and twisted his hair in a frenzy during the heat of student arguments in the Bun Room.

The voice was gentle and well bred, though rather desperate as he sat down heavily on a sooty wall top and said to the cat, 'What the hell is the point of it all, cat? Just what the hell is the point of it all? One is expected to qualify, to find gainful employment, to marry and breed from a nagging wife, to put up with squalling brats, to pay income tax, to grow old, draw one's pension and die. Just what *is* the point of it all?'

50

The cat sniffed him, found he smelt friendly in spite of the stink of beer, and settled in his lap.

'Fat lot you care, you lucky black devil,' said the drunk. 'To be, or not to be, that is the question.' There was much more of this, but the cat did not become bored, since he couldn't understand a word of it. Warmth was flowing up into his belly nicely, from the drunk's legs. He purred.

'Cat,' said the drunk, 'you are obviously a philosopher. I shall call you Satan. Since you would obviously rather rule in Hell than serve in Heaven.' And with all the arrogance of the young, who think the whole world was created for their benefit, he picked the cat up and took him home.

The cat did not object; anything was better than this night promised to be, stuck on a brick corner while the frost deepened jut before dawn.

There was a lot of bother with latchkeys, which rather tried the cat's patience, since his head kept getting squashed in the drunk's armpit. But eventually they arrived in a room where an old gas fire burnt blue and popping, and it was warm.

The drunk collapsed on the bed, so worried about the desolate future for mankind that he instantly fell asleep and was snoring, his young cheek above the beard smooth and pink against the grey roughness of the duffle coat. The cat explored the room; the jumble of shoes and boots under the bed; the dirty shirts and sweaters straggled around the floor; the clutter of unwashed plates in the sink which yielded several bits of bacon rind, and a congealed mass of egg that the cat's rough tongue soon rasped clean.

Towards dawn, the gas meter ran out of money, the fire went out with a loud pop, and the room grew cold. The cat abandoned its place on the hearth rug, and wormed its way into the sleeping arms and folds of duffle coat, only its head exposed and its ears alert.

So, some hours later, it heard the pad of soft footsteps on the stairs outside, the chink of milk bottles at the front door, the returning soft footsteps. And smelt a whiff of human, very fresh and clean. It looked at its still-snoring host, and decided nothing was to be hoped for from that quarter for some time yet. It drew itself gently out of the encircling arms, stretched fore and aft, dropped to the floor with a soft thud, yawned, attacked one shoulder momentarily with its pink tongue, then skipped through the slightly open door and followed the footsteps.

'Hel-*lo*! What's your name, puss? Where did you come from? How did you get in here?'

His new friend was clad from neck to feet in a white padded housecoat, with little springs of dark blue flowers printed all over it. Beneath, a pair of sensible brown leather sandals peeped out. The blonde hair was pulled back viciously inside an elastic band, to make a ponytail. It gave a tightness to the skin of her cheekbones, and slightly elongated her large blue eyes, in a way that was not unflattering. Her eyes were shining, in spite of the early hour, her cheeks were rosy, and her yawn (covered delicately by the back of her hand, even in private) was one of contentment rather than weariness. She had obviously gone to bed early and slept well.

'Well, you *are* a stranger! Cats aren't allowed in this hostel. But I suppose you'd better have some milk before you go . . .'

The word 'milk' was the only one that made sense to the cat. It pricked its ears, and ran before her into the little spotless kitchen.

They sat together, on chairs each side of the tiny table, with its clean seersucker tablecloth. There was so much that was new for the cat to observe. The shiny silver coffeepot, with its intriguing smell and steam coming out of the spout. The seersucker napkin, unfolded from a silver napkin-ring. Bowl of cornflakes, pieces of neat crisp toast, the home-made marmalade in the pot with its silver holder. All this the cat observed solemnly, green eyes flitting here and there.

'You're a very *polite* cat. You're a bit like old Binkie. Except you've been fighting, you *bad* boy. I wonder if you'd let me bathe those cuts . . .'

The cat watched the piece of toast ascend to her mouth. Watched her bite off one corner with a crunch of evident enjoyment. She had nice red lips and her teeth were white and even . . .

'Oh, you poor thing, you're *hungry*. Would you like some toast? Cat's should *not* be fed at table. Oh, here you are . . .' The cat crunched the toast with great delicacy, turning its head on one side, and mopping up every crumb from the tablecloth afterwards. His hostess had turned to her diary, full of neat tiny writing in bright blue.

'The metaphysical poets, ten o'clock. Seminar, half-past eleven. Lunch with Sheila, and hockey this afternoon. And finish the essay for Simms tonight. And a nice sunny day for it. Good!' But for such an optimistic declaration, the voice was a little wistful. 'I don't know about this university lark, cat. It's all right, I suppose. But it's just like school, really. Only more spread out, which is not much fun when your bike's got a slow puncture. Oh, and the launderette – oh damn!'

When she was ready for the day, with the merest touch of lipstick and her college scarf wound bravely round her long slim white throat, she carefully locked her door and made her way downstairs. Only giving a slight shudder as she heard the snores proceeding from the darkness behind the slightly open door. Accompanied by the smell of sweaty socks and beer . . . Some people were a disgrace to the university.

Then she looked round for the cat, so she could put him back out into the world where he rightly belonged.

But the cat was nowhere to be seen. And she couldn't waste a minute, or she'd be late for her ten o'clock lecture.

That evening, the cat was waiting at her door to welcome her. She knew she ought to put him out, but it had been a disastrous day. That dreadful creature Bewdley downstairs had not only turned up late for the lecture on the metaphysicals, looking as if he'd slept in his clothes, but had spent the session asking awkward questions of Mr Simms, and had got poor Mr Simms in a right muddle. How dare Bewdley question the known facts about John

Donne; just when she'd got them down neatly in her lecture notes? Bewdley just did it to provoke; to make himself look clever in front of his horrible friends in the back row of the lecture theatre. Bewdley should be *shot* for interrupting the work of the university.

And then the seminar. Bewdley again, with his snide little cracks. Running his hands through that hair that stuck up like a birds nest. Didn't the awful creature have a comb? Bewdley turning to her, so rudely, saying in the middle of her reading out her essay, 'Do you believe *everything* the grown-ups tell you? You're not at school now, you know. Life's more than getting ten out of ten . . .' She could have *hit* him, the little weed . . . And he *smelt*.

And then Sheila, turning up for lunch with that obnoxious tart Laura Freeland, and talking about clothes nonstop. And Laura Freeland saying spitefully, 'English county women are all bum and no boobs . . .'

And they'd lost the hockey match against Durham women 4–3.

She needed a strong cup of tea. She also felt the cat was her only friend in the world. She put on the kettle and told him all about it. The cat listened gravely, lifting his cool green eyes from his saucer of milk.

Draw the curtains, shut the horrible day out. Settle by the gas fire with the table pulled close, and the cat dozing on it. The cat calmed her. She thought of the things that creep Bewdley had said, and suddenly she saw his arguments were false. Well, not *entirely* false; but she saw two places where she could trip him up. She carefully looked up the references in the book. That was just like Bewdley; lots of flashy clever arguments, but hadn't bothered to do his homework on them. She wrote against Bewdley, seeing his sneering dark face in front of her, and she wrote with unusual spirit. Everything seemed to come together, when she argued with Bewdley in her mind. She finished, looked up at her little travelling clock and saw it was midnight. God, the time had flown! It had been *exciting*. As it had never been before. She looked forward to seeing Bewdley's face at the next seminar . . .

She looked at the cat, and the cat looked at her. Feeling for once wise and powerful, she imposed the wisdom and power on the cat.

'They ought to call you Solomon,' she said. 'I am black but comely, o ye daughters of Jerusalem,' and giggled.

She wondered what to do with the cat. It seemed cruel to just chuck him out into the night, when he'd helped her so much. But he'd been indoors at least eight hours . . . he must want to . . .

The cat solved the dilemma for her. Suddenly, its ears gave one twitch and it ran to the door and demanded to be out.

Wise beast . . .

The cat flew downstairs, and was waiting by the front door as Bewdley's fumbling key scratched at the lock.

'Hello, Satan,' said Bewdley. 'What's all the hurry? Oh . . .' He waited, tolerantly while the cat prowled and sniffed, selecting a certain discreet place behind a lump of gaunt privet. He was in a good mood; he'd had a good day. Starting with putting that blonde bitch upstairs in her place. Stuck-up and cool with it. One of Nature's Head Girls, with her neat little notebook. Nice legs, though. Nice altogether, if you liked the Amazon type . . .

When it was finished, the cat followed him upstairs, nose working violently.

'Got you a Cornish pasty . . .'

It had fallen apart in its greasy bag, on the erratic journey home. But the cat ate every bit, then settled into the woollen mounds of the unmade bed for the night.

Two nights later, Bewdley held one of his parties. He had by far the biggest bedsit in the house, on the first floor, and made the most of it. The tones of Bewdley's record player boomed up through her floorboards and thin carpet. All peculiar records. Juliette Greco; the Rolling Stones' dangerous snarl and grumble, and the eternal whining of Ravi Shankar. The smell of joss sticks, cigarette smoke or worse came up through the cracks in her floorboards . . .

She would complain to the college authorities again.

55

But nobody else in the house would, because Bewdley cunningly asked them to his parties and they went. Some considered Bewdley smart; some considered him the college Jean-Paul Sartre, in his black polo-neck sweater rolled up to the elbows, and his black jeans. With the Gauloise hanging endlessly from the corner of his mouth, and his thin expressive hands waving in the air.

He had rather elegant hands . . . she stuffed down the thought. Bewdley was a louse, a worm, a . . .

She banged savagely on the floor, with the end of her hockey stick. A roaring jeer from the partygoers rose through the floorboards in retaliation. They really hated her. To them she was a monster.

She was *not* a monster . . .

She was just about to push her head under the pillows, so they wouldn't hear the sound of her weeping, when there came a scratching on the door. In a sudden red rush of rage, she answered it, quite determined to knock somebody's head from their shoulders.

But it was only Solomon, tail raised in greeting. She picked him up and cuddled him. But he struggled out of her arms, and ran off downstairs. He must want to be let out . . . She followed him shrinkingly, past the riotous door. As she passed it, something or somebody hit the panels of the door with a terrible thump, and there was another roar of jeering laughter above the whining music. But, thank God, the door didn't open.

In the hall, Solomon didn't immediately want to go out. He sniffed at the cupboard under the stairs. Suddenly curious, in the middle of her distressed weariness, she had the urge to look inside. Maybe there was a cellar down there, blessed quiet . . .

But there was only the electricity fusebox . . .

A sudden demon seized her. The fuses were clearly labelled. That one marked 'First Floor' . . .

She pulled it out swiftly. Loosened one end of the fuse-wire, so it was useless, but still looked in place, and slammed it back, and closed the cupboard door.

Upstairs, the whine of Ravi Shankar had died. She

heard somebody yell, 'Your poxy record player's conked out, Bewdley!'

Oh, glory. They hadn't even spotted it was the power supply! They must be sitting in candlelight, like they always did. Candles stuck in old Chianti bottles. Très, très chic! Drunken idiots!

She looked round for Solomon (blessing him for saving her from a sleepless night, in his wisdom) but he was nowhere to be seen. Thankfully and silently, she tiptoed past the accursed door and back to bed.

Meanwhile, Solomon had scratched at the accursed door, and been admitted, to great welcoming shouts of 'Satan, Satan' and 'Let's have a black mass!'

But somehow, with the departure of Ravi Shankar, the spirit of partygoing had also departed. Bewdley started an argument about the philosophical theories of Dr John Wisdom that soon emptied the room of everyone except his physicist crony Jack Nida.

Solomon-Satan thankfully made his nest by pawing the rumpled bed and settled down for an overdue sleep.

A week later, she decided she had reached a crossroads with Solomon. She must either chuck him out for good, or report him to the college authorities, or adopt him. And then she realised she couldn't possible chuck him out into tonight's blizzard. And if she reported him, they would probably take him away and have him put down . . . So, it was adoption. But what would happen to him when she went down at the end of term?

She would take him home. Mummy wouldn't mind. Mummy loved cats. He'd be a friend for Binkie – they'd make a lovely pair – two matched black cats playing together. And he was so sweet and well-behaved, he wouldn't even need to be neutered . . . she would have to buy him a collar and medal.

Meanwhile, downstairs, Satan was presiding over a meeting of six who were busy proving to a luckless member of the Student Christian Movement (female) that God was redundant, non-existent, or at least if he existed, the kind of God that pulled wings off flies for enjoyment.

There was a roar of triumph as the Christian, in the face of Bewdley's last argument, lost her faith altogether, and departed with her treacherous boyfriend in such a state of turmoil that her seduction that night was a foregone conclusion. The black cat rose, yawned and stretched.

'Wicked little devil, isn't he?' asked Bewdley admiringly. 'You'd think he'd understood every word. We really must have a black mass sometime . . .'

The seminar when she read her counterblast to Bewdley had gone with amazing success. Two of her arguments had gone home like torpedoes and blown his clean out of water. One of Bewdley's friends had turned on him and said, 'Talk your way out of that one, Bewdley!'

And all Bewdley could think of by way of reply was some mumble about not having the time to read the literary small print. Then, oddly, *everyone* had turned on him. Even nice kindly Mr Simms had said that Bewdley was reducing his first-class academic mind to a pulp with booze.

Bewdley wasn't half so popular or so fearsome as she'd thought. People didn't so much like him as suck up to him, because they were scared of him.

Very satisfying. Bewdley had looked so pale and lost she had almost felt sorry for him.

On the way home, she had stopped off at the pet shop and collected the collar and medal for Solomon. He had just strolled out wearing it, as proud as Punch.

She was about to make herself a cup of tea, when there came a thunderous knocking on the door. A knocking that was so rude, it made her angry before she opened it.

It was Bewdley. Holding Solomon.

'What the hell do you mean?' he shouted. 'Solomon? He's called Satan. He's *my* bloody cat. *I* feed him.'

'On *what*? Beer?' She was in no mood to take any nonsense from Bewdley.

'Pies. Cornish pasties. From the Bun Room.'

'Pies? Cornish *pasties*? What kind of food value have

58

they got? He gets Kit-e-Kat here. I wouldn't trust you with a pet *mouse*. Give him to *me*!'

'Gerroff!' roared Bewdley, his gift for fine language for once deserting him. They rocked from side to side, locked in mortal combat. Solomon-Satan, eyes wide, ears back, made a frantic leap from Bewdley's arms, and landed on the top of her wardrobe. It was then that she realised that she was not only a centimetre taller than Bewdley, but considerably stronger. She gave him a furious push, and he staggered right across the room, banged his head on a cupboard handle and collapsed unconscious on the floor.

She knelt over him. What slender bones he had! A nose like a little hawk. And such long beautiful eyelashes closed over his unconscious eyes. And such a smooth fine skin . . . With him unconscious, and herself frantic, she suddenly saw what Bewdley's women saw in Bewdley. The lost little boy who rode on the back of the monster and couldn't get down even if he wanted to.

At that moment, Bewdley opened his eyes, and saw hers, enormous with alarm and candid with decency and caring, staring down at him. He was *enchanted*. But all he said, being Bewdley, was, 'I think you've cracked my skull open.'

'Nonsense! I've had worse cracks than that on the hockey field.'

'My legs don't seem to work,' said Bewdley, cunningly. 'And I'm seeing everything double!'

'Concussion!' Suddenly alarmed again, and eminently practical, she picked him up bodily and laid him on the couch.

Bewdley lay still, with his eyes shut, glorying in the memory of the round strength of her arms around his thin body, and the warmth and size of her bosom.

She got him upright eventually, with the threat of calling a doctor and a hot cup of tea. But neither of them were quite the same as before.

She told herself that all he needed was firmly taking in hand. He must have been neglected as a child . . .

He told himself he had always admired big women.

59

And he'd never had a genuine blonde, only the bottle variety . . .

There was never, in that university, a more ill-matched couple, a stranger love affair. Like a crocodile and a giraffe taking a smit on each other.

She wanted him, because he felt *dangerous*. Her life was too well-organised, and she was bored. He was her new Nook's Cave.

Years ago, when only a kid, she had taken to walking to Nook's Cave at dusk. Through the dark gnarled old oaks of Nook's Wood to its centre, where a tiny sandstone ridge thrust its way up through the leaf mould, and set in the ridge, a deep low dank dark cave. There was never anybody in the wood; there was never anything in the cave. But she always approached it with her legs shaky with delicious terror, and she always left it with a feeling of profound relief, tinged with a profound disappointment. She still did it sometimes in the holidays; she had never worked out what she went looking for.

She brought back his childhood, too. A childhood of clean beds and clean shirts every day, where his mother kept everything proper. He had escaped into a self-made world of unmade beds and roisterous nights and booze, of which he was getting rather tired. But he'd made his image with his gang, and he was trapped in it, until she came along.

She told herself he was her little weakness; something on the side, to be picked up and tossed down as she liked. He told himself the same thing about her. They hid each other from their friends, mildly ashamed of each other. They met in the gaps of their *real* week; between getting home in the afternoon, and going out in the evening. On once-dreary Sunday afternoons.

The cat kept them in touch. The cat was delighted his two persons were getting together, getting affectionate. He trotted from one room to the other; they took to sending each other tiny scribbled messages, tucked into his collar. When they sat close, on her window seat, or in his sagging armchairs each side of the popping feeble gas fire, he sat between them and purred. They had settled his name, by a miracle of compromise that pleased them both. Alone, she still called him Solomon; alone, he still called him Satan. Together, they called him 'S' or 'Ess'. He answered to everything; to him the sounds just meant there was food in the offing, or affection.

They sat drinking tea in her room from delicate bone china; or coffee in his room from dark and dubious mugs. He built exciting castles in the air, trying to prove that all human goodness was an illusion, or that God did not exist. She waited patiently for his first false move, his first wrong fact or misquotation, and brought his houses of cards tumbling down.

'God, you're a dull factual sod,' he would say with grudging admiration, and they would both laugh.

It was the happy time.

And then, such is the sinful world, they began to try to change each other. One evening, her elaborate hairstyle lost a couple of hairpins and began to fall down. He pulled out the rest of the pins and her hair streamed down golden and straight, and he said it made her look sexy, like Minou Drouet, who worked the cabarets on the Left Bank in Paris. She took to wearing her hair loose.

He told her that black would suit her blondeness; in an idle moment, shopping, she tried on a black polo-neck sweater, and then a black leather skirt, and finished it off with black shoes and a pair of black nylons. From being a despised games-playing hearty round the college, she began to draw wolf whistles . . .

In turn, she counter-attacked on his untidiness. Insisted on washing up his filthy mugs; objected to the layer of congealed fat in his kitchen frying pan. One long wet Sunday evening, when they had been too long together, and the musky smell of him was getting under her skin in a way she found disturbing, she rounded on him and screamed that if he didn't go and have a bath, she wouldn't even *kiss* him. He turned very pale, told her to go to hell, and stormed out, slamming the door behind him. That might have been the end of it, except the cat kept on padding between them, as they sat and lay staring at a new and dreadful loneliness; a cat smelling of her eau de Cologne, and his Gauloises . . . Unable to bear it, she slipped a note in the cat's collar, inviting him to tea. He turned up with his hair wet from a bath, and she combed it for him; then, greatly daring, trimmed his beard. As he stood so patiently enduring the scissors, she felt her heart turn over.

But she refused to sleep with him. She doubted he could keep his mouth shut if she did. And Girls Who Did definitely got gossiped about in that college. And there were at least three other girls here from her old school who'd be only too eager to write home to their parents . . .

He raged on at her that he couldn't work for thinking about it. She replied *she* could work very well (though at times she did find such thoughts a great distraction). He screamed she was ruining his health. She replied she was not the National Health Service and he could go and find a female consultant among his ex-women.

He said he bloody well would and goodbye, and slammed out again. That silence lasted an agonising week, during which she writhed on her bed in agony, full of thoughts of him with other women. But she would *not* give in. The Girls Who Did frequently lost their blokes anyway, and went to bits and couldn't work, and got sent down. And she wanted her good second-class degree and a career.

It might have ended *there*. But one night he knocked on her door, looking very vulnerable and worried, and said the cat was ill. It had been sick three times yesterday and now it wouldn't eat or even drink. She ran downstairs. Ess was hunched up on the unmade bed, looking very sorry for himself, with a nose as dry and rough as old leather. His tummy was swelled up and hard, and he yowled a bit as she picked him up. All their old enmity drowned in a mutual sea of panic. Together they bored air holes in Bewdley's old battered suitcase, and went out into the cold streets of the city to find a vet.

It took till nearly ten o'clock, before they tracked down

a vet who gave Ess an injection, filled a packet with tablets, and told them Ess would live.

As they got on the bus, limp with relief, he said, 'Come down to the Bun Room for a drink?'

Gay with relief, she said, 'Why not?', though she had never been in that existentialist den of vice in her innocent college life.

The end of the evening was a great success. The cat in the suitcase was greeted as a very suitable Bewdley eccentricity. Ess, rapidly recovering, sat on the beer-soaked piano while it was being played, ate a Cornish pasty with reviving interest and even sipped delicately from a half-full beer mug.

She was very much admired in her black gear (which she had been wearing in a fit of nostalgia for Bewdley). It was quite clear, from the looks and mutters of Bewdley's gang that he *had* discussed their limited sex life, widely. And she had become that most desirable of creatures, the Girl Who'd Been Asked and Who Wouldn't.

And when Trillack, in a bravura attempt to gain attention, tried to disprove the existence of the Historical Jesus (a trick of which all Bewdley's mates were totally sick) she shot him down with quotations from Josephus and Tacitus and Pliny, and forced him into the ridiculous position of trying to prove the existence of Julius Caesar instead. Which attempt she demolished with Trillack's own arguments. All but Trillack agreed it was very elegant. Ess beamed down at her from the piano.

But it wasn't until they were walking home, carrying Ess in the suitcase between them, that she realised what had made the evening so totally fantastic.

Bewdley had acknowledged her as his woman. In front of all his gang. Even when everybody knew that, for the first time in Bewdley's career, she was the Girl Who Wouldn't.

She still Wouldn't. Though they often ended up an evening half-dressed, she on the bed, he hunched in a chair, glaring at each other like caged tigers.

She tried to make up for it by growing maternal about him. She offered to wash his shirts and socks. Bewdley

63

went pale, with a bottled-up mixture of independence, fury and distress.

She said gently, 'It will save a lot of time doing up parcels!' She had long known that, in desperation, he sent huge ill-wrapped brown-paper parcels of washing home to his mother, creeping surreptitiously down College Street with them to the post office in the Haymarket, when he thought none of his mates would be about. The parcels frequently came open in the post; he lost a lot of beloved black socks that way.

With a mute nod, head down, he capitulated, and her heart sang. She took him down to the first launderette to open in the town, and showed him how to cope, and they held hands and watched the black stuff swirling round in its dark grey suds. That night, she was so overcome with maternal feelings for him, she very nearly Did. They lay very close a very long time, and Ess came and sat on her naked hip, purring, as if he was king of the castle, and totally approved.

But she pushed things too far. One evening, when he was up in the library book-stack, swotting hard and late for his finals, she wandered in through his half-open door in a mood of sentimental longing.

The room was in an even worse state than usual. Out of sheer love, she washed the pots, picked up jumpers. Then passion really took hold of her, so that to work off her feelings she set to and cleaned the room from top to bottom.

And found something quite unforgiveable under the bed. Black, with lace edging, and definitely *not* hers. She sat on long in a fury, in the straight tidy room, and finally departed, leaving the unmentionable lying right in the middle of the immaculate bed. Very quietly, she cried. herself to sleep.

At midnight, there was a thunderous knocking at her door, and she had to let him in, or he'd have had the whole house roused. Once inside, he held the unmentionable under her nose, and said it had nothing to do with him; he'd lent his room to Trillack last Wednesday when he was working late, and the unmentionable belonged to

June Schofield, and it was entirely Trillack's responsibility and he'd wring the little bastard's neck personally.

She had to believe him; but before she could even start to apologise, he began going on about her taking liberties and making his room unbearable and destroying his sense of his own existence, and besides he couldn't find his essay on Marlowe's *Edward the Second* anywhere.

She tried to tell him she'd done it all for love, but it came out as a weak bleat, and he immediately roared past her bleats saying love was crap invented by women to enslave men and she couldn't *bear* him going on like that and she put her arms around him and . . .

They slept at last, looking as totally rosy and innocent as the Babes in the Wood, and Ess slept on top of the heap, bathing his black being in the vibes of his happy humans.

She felt uneasy, vulnerable, all that June; but it seemed to be, by chance's arbitrary whim, happy-endings time. She learnt she was out of the wood the day Bewdley's Finals result came out, and he got his First.

He seemed to feel the change that month more than her. He had given up drink and the Bun Room altogether (but that might have been because of Finals). He bought a decent suit (but that might have been for graduation, and because he was starting to get job interviews). He became sober and clean and properly dressed, so she began to wonder if she'd caught a true tiger after all. He was so solicitous, almost sentimental. They walked Ess in Leazes Park, hand-in-hand under the trees, like any other respectable about-to-be-engaged pair. He took her home to meet his parents, between the exam and the results coming out, and that decent and intelligent couple seemed to like her and be very relieved that he hadn't brought home something infinitely worse. Bewdley even agreed to face *her* parents after the results . . .

But on the night the results came out, they met Trillack, who had got a poor Second, but insisted very decently that they celebrate Bewdley's First. How could they refuse such selfless magnanimity?

The moment they entered the Bun Room, she smelt the disaster in the air. All the gang were there, and the gang had not forgiven her for stealing Bewdley from them, and the gang wanted Bewdley back before they lost him altogether. The talk was especially wild and vicious, and concerned with heredity and environment. Bewdley went back to his old stance of being a child of the workers, son of a black-faced fitter. And now she knew that his father was a rather well-paid works engineer, it seemed to ring particularly false. Why did he have to *pretend* so? What was wrong with being the son of a well-paid engineer? What was there to be ashamed of? Why was he being so *childish*?

And then they began getting at her, with snide questions about horse riding and point-to-point races, and fox-hunting being the unspeakable in pursuit of the uneatable. She had never been keen on hunting, though she loved horses, but the attacks on her own sort of people were so unfair, she felt her face going red.

Then Jack Nida spoke up from the corner, trying to make peace. She'd always liked Nida; he was the brightest of the gang, a physicist, a gentle-faced Jew. The only one of the lot with decency and kindness in him, and a bad stammer . . .

'You can overcome both your b-b-birth and your upbringing by will and logic,' said Nida. 'I was b-b-born a Jew, but now, see, I am an atheist. I am f-f-free of my heredity.'

'Like hell you are,' said Bewdley. And suddenly it was the old Bewdley talking again, the black monster she had thought was gone forever.

'You have my word for it. I am an atheist. I believe the world was created by chance.' Nida laid his hand on his red shirt, quivering with gentle earnestness. 'I *swear* it.'

'Would you pee against the wall of a synagogue?' asked Trillack, and there was a nasty laugh.

'My friend, I would not pee against the wall of a synagogue or the wall of a church, or the wall of a mosque. I am a civilised person. Why should I offend others, however mistaken their beliefs?'

It silenced them, with its very decency. She was seized with a great love for Nida; she felt like taking him in her arms. How gentle he would be! What a father he would make . . .

It might have been that Bewdley caught her traitorous look, and that was what made him do it.

'Just a minute,' he said. Got up and crossed the Bun Room to the bar and counter, and bought something on a plate. When he came back, she saw it was a meat pie, the usual sort. She was just baffled. The harmlessness of Bewdley's action did not go with the diabolical look on his face.

Bewdley put the pie in front of Nida. Nida looked up at him with gentle enquiry.

'If you're not a Jew,' said Bewdley, 'eat it.' Then he added, 'It's *pork*.'

She would never forget the look on Nida's face. Or the way he crossed the room, and got a knife, and cut the pie into small pieces, and began to eat it, delicately as a cat. Or the pale quiet way he sat afterwards.

Or the way he suddenly put his hand over his face, and got up and ran from the room. Or the way he spewed up helplessly in the doorway. Or the thunderous roar of triumph and laughter from the gang.

Somebody else had to clear it up. She ran up the steps and outside, but Nida was nowhere to be seen. She kept walking.

Bewdley came home, half an hour later. He knocked on her door and asked very quietly to come in. He was nervous, and didn't look at her, as she sat quietly nursing Ess on her lap.

'Look,' he said finally, still not looking at her. 'It was only a joke . . .'

'Not for Nida.'

His voice rose in its unattractive whine. 'Look, he asked for it. Making out he was so high and mighty.'

'He was your friend. He wouldn't have done that to you. Humiliating him in front of everybody . . .'

'It was the *truth*! He was talking crap, and I proved it to him. We got at the *truth*!'

'So truth's worth more than friendship?'

'Yes,' he shouted. '*Yes*!'

'Goodbye, Bewdley,' she said quietly. But with total conviction.

'But *why*?' He believed her; his voice rose to a shriek of panic.

'Because one day you might prefer the truth to *me*. In public.'

'It's not like that!'

'It is.' Her voice was so steely, the cat shifted uneasily on her knee.

She finished him with those two words. All he could think of to say was, 'How about Ess?'

'He goes home with me, at the end of term. Otherwise, you might prefer the truth to *him*, one day.'

And that was the end of them.

She bought a new basket specially, to take Ess home in. She still has him; though he is old now, and doesn't go out much. Still, when Bewdley appears on the South Bank Show, tearing some new artistic enterprise to pieces, she gives Ess that understanding smile.

Of escape and relief.

EAST DODDINGHAM DINAH

East Doddingham Dinah was never a ghost; at least till the end.

She was a living cat; yet as near a ghost as a living cat can be. Long white fur and pale blue eyes. When she let you pick her up (which wasn't often) you'd realise half of her was fur. Only deep inside that luxurious fur you'd feel thin bones and thinner muscles, frail as wire. She hardly weighed a thing. All soul, she was; a loving soul looking out of huge dark unfathomable eyes, set in a head like a beautiful white skull. I never saw a cat that could jump like her; she could almost fly, like the frail thin aeroplanes she loved.

East Doddingham? East Doddingham was a World War II bomber airfield, set in the bleak wastes of Lincolnshire. The evening Dinah arrived, it was under a shroud of snow and thin fog, so it's no puzzle why the ground-crews never saw her.

She was looking for warmth, like the rest of us. But she didn't, like any ordinary cat, make for the glowing stoves of the Nissen huts, or the greasy delights of the cookhouse. She must have climbed up the ladder into B-Baker, on the dispersal pad.

She must have made herself snug in the best place; the rest bed that's halfway down the tail, towards the rear gun turret. Rest bed they called it; that was a laugh. Who can rest on a bombing mission? The rest bed is where we put the dying and the dead; the snug-looking red blankets don't show the blood.

Anyway, the neatly folded piles of blankets were good enough for Dinah. She must have buried herself in them; nobody noticed her till after take-off.

If we'd obeyed orders, she'd have soon been dead. We

69

were supposed to fly at 26,000 feet where the Jerry night fighters couldn't get at us so easily. At 26,000 feet there's so little air her lungs would have burst. But I followed the gospel according to Mickey Martin. 7,000 feet, where the light anti-aircraft guns are out of range, and the big ones can't draw a bead on you quick enough. I'd followed the gospel according to Mickey Martin for a year; Mickey was still alive, and so was I.

But it's still bitterly cold at 7,000, and it must have been the cold that drove her out. She made for the nearest human she could smell; who was Luke Goodman our rear gunner. Luke had left his armoured doors a touch open, and she slipped through and on to his lap as if he was sitting by his own fireside. How can she have known that, of all of us, Luke was the one who was mad about cats?

Anyway, Luke had a lot to offer her, besides his lap. He'd shoved the nozzle of the hot-air hose down his right flying boot, so the air would flow up nicely round his crotch. So Dinah got the full benefit. And of course he was starting to nibble nervously at his huge greasy pack of corned beef sandwiches . . . And in return she rubbed her white head against his face, and kept him nicely insulated where it mattered most. The pair of them must have been in Heaven. Until Luke hit his first problem.

We were over the North Sea by that time; time to test his guns. He put it off as long as he could; scared the din would frighten her away. But in the end, those twin Brownings are all that stands between a tail-end-Charlie and a nasty end splattered all over the inside of his turret. So he fired them.

She didn't flinch an inch; only watched the lines of red tracer flying away behind with an interested lift of her head. It was then he realised that, being white with blue eyes, she was stone deaf, of course. How else could she have borne the endless deafening roar of the engines without going mad?

Anyway, quite oblivious of all this, I made landfall on the enemy coast; picked up the island of Texel, and headed in over the Zuyder Zee. Not much flak that way in, except for a few useless flak ships. But Jerry put up quite a pretty display as we passed between Arnhem and Nijmegen. Luke told me afterwards that Dinah was fascinated, her head darting this way and that, following every flash and line of tracer. She didn't shiver; she sort of quivered with excitement, sometimes dabbing out a paw as if to catch the red and yellow slow-floating balls.

Frankly, when he told me afterwards, I broke out in a cold sweat . . . If he was so busy playing with that damned cat, how could he possibly have his eyes skinned for night fighters? On the other hand, she was at least keeping him awake. For the danger is not the flak, not at our height. But the quiet bits between, when you seem to be flying alone through an empty moonlit sky, and the war might be on another planet. That's when rear gunners actually fall asleep through cold and loneliness and boredom, and the weariness after terror. As skipper, I had to keep on yakking at them, down the intercom, nagging them like a wife, asking if their nose is running or their feet are freezing. Anything to keep them awake. For it's in the peace and moonlit quiet that the night fighters come. Creeping in beneath your belly till they're only fifteen metres away, and they can't possibly miss with their fixed upward-pointing cannons.

Anyway, in the quiet bit before we hit the Ruhr, or Happy Valley as we called it, Luke said he was wide awake, and so was Dinah, just purring like a little engine. He couldn't hear her, of course, but he could feel her throat vibrating against his knee.

Then suddenly, she seemed to see something he couldn't. She tensed, flicked her head from side to side, as if to get a better view, then dabbed out swift as lightning with her right paw, against the perspex of the turret window.

Luke looked where she'd dabbed; but he couldn't see a bloody thing.

She tensed and dabbed out again. And still he couldn't see anything. He began to wonder if it wasn't one of those tiny black flies you get in Lincolnshire, the ones cats chase when you think they're chasing nothing.

And then she dabbed again; and he saw it. Even smaller than a fly on the perspex. A grey shape against the clouds below that could only be a Jerry. Out of range, but hoping to creep up beneath us. Luke was the first to admit that, without Dinah, he'd never have seen it. But now he had seen it, he had the edge; he felt like God, with Dinah on his knee. Invincible.

So he didn't warn me, like he should have done. He just eased his turret round ever so slowly, so that Jerry wouldn't spot that he'd been lumbered. Got Jerry in his ring-sight and watched him grow.

Luke said the Jerry was one of the best, a real craftsman. Took advantage of every bit of cloud to climb, get a bit nearer. Soon Luke could see he was an ME 110, with more radar antennae bristling on its nose than a cat's got whiskers. No front guns to worry about, then: only the fixed upward-pointing cannons behind the cockpit that Jerry couldn't use until he was directly under our belly . . .

Luke waited; waited until he could see the black mottle on its grey wings; waited until he could almost read its serial number, till he could see the white face of the pilot looking upwards. Then he gave it a five-second burst, right into the cockpit. He said the cockpit flew apart in a shower of silver rain; but the thing went on flying steadily beneath us. Perhaps the pilot was already dead. But he gave it another five-second burst into the right engine, and the fire grew . . .

I nearly had a heart attack. Luke screaming, 'I've got him, skipper, I've *got* him.' And suddenly this Jerry in flames appeared directly underneath my nose, so I had to throw the crate upwards and to port, to avoid going with it, when it blew up . . .

I can tell you, the bomb run over Dusseldorf was an anti-climax after that. And the run home was like a party. Because it's not often that a rear gunner gets a night fighter in our lot. I mean, imagine standing on a railway-station platform at night, with kids throwing burning fireworks at you, and a train comes through at a hundred miles an hour and you've got to hit the fat man sitting in

the third compartment of the . . .
air pistol . . . that's what it's like be.
only got a Jerry once before; in the ea.,
bemused waist gunner in a Wimpey, in .
Berlin, saw a Messerschmidt 109, without radar,
a clue, poor sod, sail past his gun at less than a hun.
yards range, overtaking a bomber he never even saw. The
gunner was so amazed he almost missed the shot. But not
quite. The Jerry went down without ever knowing what
hit him. But that was the only other time we got one.

But now, my lot thought we were the greatest; thought
we were invincible. I was in a cold sweat all the way
home, trying to get them to go on keeping a close lookout.

But it wasn't till we crossed the Dutch coast that Luke
said he had a cat sitting on his knee.

'Poor sod,' said Hoppy the wireless op, over the intercom. 'Greatness hath made him mad.' Hoppy did a year
at Oxford, before he volunteered to be a coconut shy at
26,000 feet over the Ruhr. He hoped to return to complete
a degree in English Literature. He may yet make it, if he
can find a way to write, with no hands to speak of . . .

There were lots of other witty cracks, catcalls and jeers.
But Luke insisted he had a white cat sitting on his knee.
And at 7,000 feet, no way could he be goofy through lack
of oxygen. So I sent Mike the flight engineer to go and
see. Anything goes wrong, I send the flight engineer to
go and see; if he's still alive.

Mike poked his head through Luke's armoured doors.

'Gotta cat all right,' he reported back.

'What's it doing?'

'Eating sandwiches . . .'

There never was a cat like Dinah for eating. When she
finished Luke's she walked forward and scrounged off
Hoppy and Bob the navigator, who sat together in the
middle of the plane. And when she'd finished off theirs,
she'd come walking calmly through the awful stink of the
plane's interior, the smell of sweat and puke and the spilt
Elsan, and sit on my knee and wash herself clean, while
the sun came up behind us, and the flat coast of

...re and the big tower of Wainfleet All Saints came pinkly out of the morning mist like the kingdom of Heaven.

She clung round Luke's neck all during debriefing, digging her claws into his old leather jacket. We were the last home, and the other crews usually hang around the debriefing hall, drinking their breakfast, which is supposed to be coffee but is usually stronger. Everybody gathered round open-mouthed. The little WAAF Intelligence officer just didn't know what to write down; she thought Luke was having her on about Dinah and the ME 110. So she summoned her Senior Man, and he summoned Groupie.

Groupie, or Group Captain Leonard Roy to you, ran our lot. Grey as a badger and too fat to get into a Wimpey, but no fool. He knew that cats shooting down ME110s was against King's Regulations. But he also weighed up the sea of grinning faces. There hadn't been many grins round East Doddingham that winter. We'd lost a lot of planes, we were permanently frozen day and night, on the ground and in the air, the local pubs were hovels, and the most attractive local females were the horses. But above all, we were the forgotten men.

You see, Wimpeys, or Wellington bombers to you, were good old crates that took a lot of knocking out of the air. But they were old, and slow. Not as slow as Stirlings, thank God, that lumbered round the air like pregnant cows, and were Jerry's favourite food. Everybody cheered when they heard the Stirlings were going on an op, because it gave the rest of us a better chance of getting home. But a Wimpey only carries a tiny bomb load. One Lancaster carries as many bombs as five Wimpeys. Why put thirty Wimpey blokes up for the chop, when seven guys in a Lanc can do the same damage (or lack of it)?

But the great British public had to have its thousand-bomber raids on Happy Valley, so we were always sent in to make up the thousand . . .

Anyway, Groupie looks around all the happy faces and says, 'Put the cat on the crew roster. Shilling a day for aircrew rations. These damn Wimpeys are always full of mice . . .'

It got a laugh; though everybody knew no mouse that valued its life would go near a Wimpey, corned beef crumbs or no corned beef crumbs.

She slept with Luke; she ate with Luke. Though in the mess hall, during an ops breakfast, she'd jump from table to table and get spoiled rotten with bacon rind and even whole bloody lumps of bacon. Because every other crew wanted her, especially after she helped Luke get his second Jerry. Aircrews were mascot-mad, you see. I mean, our last Wingco wouldn't *fly* without his old golf umbrella stuck behind his seat. He made a joke of it, of course, saying he could use it if his parachute failed to open. But the night his groundcrew mislaid it, just before a raid, he went as white as a sheet, and threw up right there on the tarmac. He still went on the raid; but he didn't come back. I saw him buy it with a direct flak hit, over the marshalling yards at Hamm. None of his crew got out.

We all had something. Hoppy had a rabbit's foot. Mike had a very battered golliwog. Bob had a penknife, with all the paint worn off, where he turned it over and over in his pocket during a raid.

But all the attempts to get Dinah away from Luke failed. Even the kidnap attempt by G-George. Dinah had been missing all day, before that night. We'd had to practically carry Luke out to the plane, because he was quite certain that without her, we were for the chop. Then, as we were waiting our turn in the queue for take-off, we saw G-George taxiing past, trying to jump the queue. That was their undoing. We saw it all quite clearly, because it was bright moonlight. Wimpeys have these little triangular windows all along their sides. Dinah's little white face appeared at one of them. And those windows are just celluloid. We saw her white paws scrabbling, then the window was out, and she leapt down and ran to us like a Derby winner. Luke, warned over the intercom, swung his turret hard left, exposing the armoured doors behind him. He opened the doors and she jumped in, and he closed the doors and swung the turret back, and we were off to Essen.

She got her third Jerry that night. After that, the Ministry of Information let in the reporters and photographers, and the legend of East Doddingham Dinah was born, with photographs of her clinging to Luke for grim life, and daft headlines like: DODDINGHAM DINAH HUNTS THE HUN.

You'd think, the way they went on, that she and Luke had shot down half the Jerry air force. But they only got four, all told. Still, I suppose it was good for the Home Front and the War Effort. Until some nut began to write to the papers, suggesting that all rear gunners carried a cat. The Air Ministry stamped on the whole stunt after that.

But she did much more marvellous things than just helping Luke shoot down night fighters. She *knew* things. Like the night she walked aboard, and then walked off again. I was just revving up, when she went to the exit hatch and began to claw at it, and give little silent miaows through the roar of the engines, *pleading* to be out.

God, the crew went *crazy* over the intercom. Should we let her out or shouldn't we? The row got so bad they even noticed in the control tower.

We all knew what it meant. She was our luck. If she went, we were for the chop, full stop . . .

Oddly enough, it was Luke who settled it. I heard his shaking voice through my headphones, he was very Yorkshire in his agony.

'She volunteered for aircrew duties, and she can bloody volunteer out, an' all. Aah'm not tekkin' her against her will.'

And nobody stopped him, when he undid the door clips and she dropped to the ground and shot off towards the warmth of the groundcrew hut.

We took off in a silence like a funeral; we went up to seven thousand in a silence like a funeral. Then Mike, the flight engineer, glancing over my shoulder at the dials said, quietly, 'Port engine's acting up, skipper!'

Well, it was. A fraction. Temperature a degree or so too hot; losing a few revs, then gaining a few, without either of us touching the throttles. But B-Baker was old, like I said. And it was the kind of acting-up that usually stopped, if you flew on for a bit. We'd been to Berlin and back on worse. And it was certainly the kind of fault which would vanish the moment you turned back to the airfield. Leaving you with egg all over your face, and a very nasty interview with Groupie. That was always the way when a guy's nerve began to go . . . the slippery slope which ended with you lying on your bunk, gibbering like a baby under the bedclothes till they came to take you away and reduce you to the rank of AC2 and put you on cleaning the airfield bogs. Lack of Moral Fibre, they said at your court martial – LMF for short.

'*Leave* it,' I snarled at Mike.

We flew on; crossed the English coast. I could feel Mike watching that dial, over my shoulder. The rest of them were still like a funeral over the intercom.

Then Luke said, 'She always was keen to come before, skipper . . .'

And Hoppy said, 'We've done forty-two missions without a gripe. They owe us one . . .'

I turned back. Immediately, the bloody port engine settled down; and ran as sweet as a sewing machine, all the way home.

I was in Groupie's office next morning, having a strip torn off me, when we heard the bang, right through the brick walls. We ran out together. But across the airfield, on her dispersal pad, poor B-Baker was already a write-off.

The sergeant of my groundcrew had been revving up the port engine of his darling to demonstrate her innocence. When a prop blade snapped off clean at the shaft. Went through the cockpit, shaving a slice off his backside, and straight out the other side into the main petrol tank in the starboard wing. Which promptly caught fire. He got away with a well-singed skin, and one and a half

77

buttocks. He was lucky; he was on the ground at the time. In the air, we wouldn't have had a prayer . . .

We never worked out how Dinah *knew*. There were those clever-cuts who reckoned she'd felt the different vibes from the duff propellor through the pads of her paws, the moment she got on board.

We reckoned she just *knew*.

Like she knew about O-Oboe.

I mean, she was always prowling around the aircraft on their dispersal pads. As I said before, she could jump as if she could almost fly. A two-metre jump to a wing root was nothing to her. She would chat up the groundcrews as they serviced the engines, and never say no to grub (though she got no fatter). Then she would go for a trot along the top of the fuselage, or wash herself in the occasional bleak glimpse of February sun, on top of a cockpit canopy. I mean, any crate, not just our brand-new B-Baker. The other crews in the squadron liked that; they reckoned she was spreading her luck round a bit. And certainly, in her first two months with the squadron, we lost no planes at all. (Though of course the snow and fog cut our bombing missions down a lot in those two months.)

But it was different with O-Oboe. Next to us, Dinah was fonder of Pip Percival's crew than any other. She was always running round O-Oboe. It was parked next to us at dispersals.

It happened after breakfast one morning. O-Oboe's groundcrew sergeant came into my little squadron office, looking . . . upset.

'I think Dinah's ill, sir. She's sitting up on O-Oboe, an' she won't come down, even for bacon.'

I got Luke, and we went across in my jeep. When we were still quite a way from O-Oboe, Luke whistled and said, 'Christ, look at that!'

He meant O-Oboe. Through the mist, she looked like a ghost. She looked . . . cold. She looked as if her wheels weren't really touching the ground. She looked like you could walk straight through her.

You probably think I'm talking nonsense. Surely on a misty morning, *all* the planes would look like that? But our new B-Baker next to O-Oboe looked just misty and oily and *solid*. We both knew what that ghostly look meant. O-Oboe was for the chop, on her next mission. We all got very twitchy about things like that. There were bunks where every guy who dared sleep in them got the chop straight away. There were Nissen huts where whole crews who dared live in them got the chop straight away. After a while, nobody would sleep in those particular bunks. After a while, a wise wing commander would turn that Nissen hut over to storing NAAFI supplies. There was even a beautiful WAAF on the station, all of whose boyfriends got the chop. Nobody would go near her. In the end, in despair, she got herself pregnant by a local farmer; as he married her, it was a happier ending than most . . .

Anyway, we knew O-Oboe was for it. And on top of O-Oboe, on the cockpit canopy, Dinah was sitting. Not washing herself as usual, but sitting hunched-up, eyes shut, ears down, forehead wrinkled. We called up to her; she never stirred. She must have been there for hours; there were beads of mist on the tips of her fur.

Luke climbed slitheringly up and got her. He wouldn't have done it for anything but Dinah. Nobody even wants to *touch* an aircraft that's due for the chop . . .

She was shivering. We took her into the squadron office and warmed her at the stove, and checked that all her legs worked and she wasn't hurt. We warmed up the milk ration, and she drank that. Her nose as cold and wet. She seemed quite normal. So we let her out . . .

She went straight back to O-Oboe, sitting in the same place.

Luke fetched her back four more times. And each time she went back. In the end, Luke said, 'She's not ill. She's just *grieving*. For O-Oboe.'

After that, we kept her shut up in a cupboard, with a blanket, till take-off. But it was too late. Word had got around. Nobody looked at O-Oboe's crew during the briefing. A sort of space opened up around them, at ops breakfast (which, confusingly, we eat at night, just before take-off). You could tell they knew they'd had it.

They didn't come back. Crews who know they're for the chop never come back.

After that, the groundcrews took against Dinah. When she appeared round their aircraft when they were servicing it, they shooed her away. She didn't understand, and kept coming back. They began throwing things at her. From being the queen of the wing, she'd become the angel of death. The first we knew of it was when she came into my office limping, with one ear torn, and her back soaked with dirty engine oil. Luke spent a whole day cleaning her up. But we didn't dare let her out of my office any more; till it was time to go on a mission.

And the new Wingco told me she'd have to go. Our losses were starting to climb again, because the weather was better, and we were flying more missions. But the wing as a whole blamed Dinah; Dinah had turned against them, and was bringing bad luck. Some bastard tried running her down with a jeep in the dark, as she was actually following us across the runway to B-Baker . . .

Luke took her to live with his aunty in Doncaster; I drove them across in the jeep. We sneaked out and left her lying asleep by a roaring fire, with a saucer of milk by her nose. We were sad, but she'd be safe there, and she'd done her bit for the War Effort.

Half an hour after we left, she vanished through aunty's open bathroom window. Two nights later, she turned up at dispersal, in time for the flight. Forty miles of strange countryside she'd crossed, in two days. And spot on time for the op.

It was to be her last op. The funny thing was, she walked aboard as calm as ever . . .

A new target. The U-boat pens at L'Orient, on the French coast. Should have been an easy one – over the sea all the way, after going as far as Land's End to confuse the German radar. Then into the top end of the Bay of Biscay, and on to L'Orient at zero height from the sea.

Jerry had Junkers 88s out over the bay, waiting for us.

Ours came in from above, for a change. If Dinah hadn't made the most incredible leap off Luke's knee to touch the top of his turret, he'd never have seen the one that nearly got us. But Luke didn't waste his chance. The bastard made off for home with one engine stopped, and glycol steaming from the other; I doubt he made it.

He was Dinah's fourth and last. The flak was hell over L'Orient; they were waiting for us. Thirty seconds before bombs-gone we took a 35mm cannonshell amidships. Bob was badly hurt; and Hoppy a bit, and Hoppy's radio set burst into flames. I never knew where our bombs went; probably into the local fish and chip shop. It was just good, with a fire aboard, to know they were gone. We went skidding on over France, with me shouting, 'Bail out, bail out!' and trying to make enough height so that the parachutes would open, before the plane blew up or broke in half.

Because, above all, aircrew are terrified of fire. I mean, it's one thing to die; it's another thing to burn slowly . . .

So it's all the more credit to Hoppy and Bob that they stayed and fought the blaze, fanned by a gale blowing in through the shell holes. Hoppy tried to rip the wireless set loose and throw it through the window, with his mittened hands. That's why he hasn't got much in the way of hands any more. In the end, the set burned its way through its mountings and out through the side of the crate, and all we were left with was a hurricane blowing through the fuselage, and two badly injured blokes . . . I went down to zero feet again and got out over the Bay as quickly as possible.

I was so busy trying to keep the crate in the air, and Mike was so busy getting morphine into Bob and Hoppy that we were nearly back over England before we realised that Luke hadn't said a word. I sent Mike back to look . . .

The rear turret was turned hard left. The armoured doors were open. Of Luke and Dinah there was no sign . . .

Luke had bailed out when I told him to. He was even more frightened of fire than the rest of us.

*

81

I got B-Baker down on a Coastal Command field near Land's End; but the fire had weakened the fuselage, and she broke in half on impact. Goodbye, B-Baker. Goodbye, Bob and Hoppy, for a long stay in hospital (though Bob made a good recovery eventually). Goodbye to my bomb aimer and front gunner, a kid called Harris who doesn't really come into this story. He'd bailed out through the front hatch when I told him, and finished the war in Stalag Luft XII. And goodbye, Luke and Dinah. Or so I thought.

Wingco put Bob and Hoppy in for the Air Force Cross, and sent me and Mike home for a month's leave to get over it. It was the end of April, and the nights were getting too short for raids into Germany. The crates were being changed from black night-camouflage to brown-and-green day-camouflage, and the crews were getting new training, for day-bombing and no one seemed to want two bomb-happy odds-and-sods. It's not usual for the Air Ministry to be so generous, but we'd nearly finished two tours of duty. Anyway, I had a nice time at home, doing up my parents' garden, which had gone to pot with the old man being on war work. And watching a bit of scratch county cricket, while the world got ready for D-Day without me.

I was weeding away in the back garden, hands all soil, when my mother said there was someone to see me.

It was Luke, shy and grinning as ever. Just looking a bit thin, that's all.

'Dinah?' I asked, dread in my heart, after I'd finished banging him on the back.

He grinned again. 'She's still catching up,' he said. And he told me all about it.

He'd got down safely in the chute, with Dinah clutched tight in his arms, though he almost lost her with the jerk when the chute opened. But she'd shot off immediately, when she heard people coming, on the ground.

Fortunately, they'd been decent French people, and they'd passed him on to the underground network that got British fliers safely out of the country.

He'd admitted he hadn't enjoyed the network much.

Flying crates was one thing. Walking and cycling through Occupied France, with a beret on his head, and civvy clothes was another. He'd kept his air-force tunic on, under his overcoat, but he was still scared the Jerries would shoot him as a spy if they caught him. And the endless waiting in the dark in barns and cellars . . .

It was Dinah who'd kept him going. She'd followed him all the way across France. When things got roughest, when he'd had to follow his guide past German patrols, she'd suddenly appear, poking her white head over a wall, or trotting along the road in front. Sometimes, when he had a long wait in some cellar or barn, she'd slip in to visit him. He was scared for her, too. Because the French were pretty hungry by that time, and were eating cats as a treat at Christmas. He said there wasn't another cat to be seen anywhere, and when people were offered rabbit pie in restaurants they made silent 'miaow' noises with their mouths.

But she'd stayed with him; as far as the Spanish frontier. And then the really incredible thing had happened.

The night they'd crossed into Spain, in the foothills of the Pyrenees, they'd been driven to earth by a last border patrol of German soldiers accompanied by the local Vichy policemen. Luke had lain with his cheek pressed into the earth, while the patrol passed. But the last Jerry had lingered; been suspicious of the clump of bushes Luke was lying in. Had seemed to sense, beyond all sense, that there was something alive in there. And then Luke, unable to hold his breath any longer, had taken a deep one, and made a dead twig lying underneath him snap. The Jerry had taken two paces towards the bushes, raised his rifle, called to the others . . .

When out had stepped Dinah, with even a damned mouse in her mouth.

Luke said the Jerry must've been a cat lover. He made a great fuss of Dinah, stroked her, called her 'liebling'. The other Jerries had laughed at him, then called him after them, saying they hadn't got all night.

And so Luke had passed into Spain, and then the

greater safety of Portugal. And still Dinah had been with him, at a distance.

He'd told the whole story to the British Consul in Lisbon, sure of getting Dinah a lift in the stripped-down bomber that flew the guys home.

The consul had been very snotty, and talked about rabies regulations, and refused.

Luke needn't have worried. They were halfway up Biscay before she emerged from the piled-up blankets of the crew's rest bed. And the crew, being good blokes, agreed to let her slip off at Hendon.

I looked at my watch. My parents lived 'somewhere in the home counties' as we used to say for security purposes in those days. And Hendon was only thirty miles away.

'She'll find me,' said Luke. 'You'll see!'

'Better stay here with us till she does. We don't want her having to walk all the way to East Doddingham. She'll be tired.'

I don't think either of us had the slightest doubt . . .

Early the second morning, she dropped on to Luke's bed through the open dormer window.

She should have come back to East Doddingham in triumph. You'd have thought they'd have put her story in the papers. But our old Groupie had gone where good groupies go, planning new forward air bases in the France that was soon to be liberated. There was a new Groupie that knew not Dinah. And the smell of Victory was in the air already, and with it that smell of peacetime bullshit that was the scourge of the RAF.

On the air station where she'd been queen, where they'd begged for a tuft of her fur for luck, or a carefully-hoarded dropped whisker, Dinah had become no more than a rabies risk. We offered to have a whip-round in the Wing, to pay for her to stay in quarantine. But such nonsense was not to be tolerated; there was a war to win. Dinah must be destroyed.

There wasn't time for anything subtle. We met the RAF policeman, as he carried Dinah out in a dirty great cage from the guardroom. It was quite simple. I knocked him cold, and Luke took the cage and ran.

They didn't court martial me, for striking an other-rank. Perhaps they were scared the story of Dinah would come out. They diagnosed me as suffering from combat fatigue, and I flew a desk for the rest of the war.

We had our first crew reunion in 1948. It took Hoppy that long to arrange it, when they finally stopped operating on what was left of his hands. Everybody but Luke was there. The Air Ministry was not helpful about Luke. They had finally caught up with him in 1945, when he returned home for his mother's funeral. He'd spent some time in the glasshouse, then got a dishonorable discharge.

We found him in 1950. He'd managed to get to Northern Ireland with Dinah; she'd stowed away on the Belfast-Laugharne ferry, following him as he knew she would. They walked together in the freedom of the Irish Republic. He'd found work as a farm hand, till his mother died.

He'd not seen Dinah since; though there'd been talk of a white cat that hung around the glasshouse gate. But when he finally got out, she'd gone. Tired of waiting perhaps. Or knocked down by a lorry.

The following year we decided at the reunion to drive down to East Doddingham. We wished we hadn't. God, what a mess. The guardroom was roofless. The runways were crumbling, and being used by men on Sunday afternoons to teach their wives to drive. The field itself was back under turnips, and the hangars were being used as grain stores. The RAF had found East Doddingham expendable, as it had always found us.

But Luke swore he'd seen a glimpse of Dinah. A white head peeping above the parapet of what had once been B-Baker's dispersal. Nobody else saw her; but we pretended to believe him.

Funny thing is, we've gone down to East Doddingham for our reunion ever since. God knows why. It's a dump. The accommodation in the pub is awful, and the beer still tastes like piss, as it always did.

But every year, somebody reckons that they see Dinah.

We never see her when we're all together. But there's always someone who goes for a last solitary sentimental stroll round the old field. And then they come back and say they've seen her. But she always vanishes immediately. She never comes across to say hello.

I saw a white cat myself, this year. Staring at me over the broken concrete with huge dark unfathomable eyes, set in a head like a beautiful skull. It *can't* be her; she'd be over forty years old, and no cat lives that long.

But maybe she went back to the field in 1945, when it was already running down, and nobody remained who remembered her (life was perilously short in the RAF). Maybe she lived in peace at last, and raised kittens. Maybe this was her daughter, or granddaughter.

Or maybe she was a ghost. Or maybe she just lives on in the fond memory and failing eyesight of ageing aircrew.

But she certainly wasn't a ghost in 1944.

A WALK ON
THE WILD SIDE

To live with a cat is to live with fear.

You can keep dogs safe till they die of obesity; collar-and-lead and walkies-in-the-park. But not cats; cats like a walk on the wild side.

You *can* deny cat nature. Like the childless couple down our lane, whose white Persians never leave the house except in spotless white cages for their monthly trip to the vet. Those cats sit endlessly in their upstairs bedroom window, staring out at the moving world, sometimes raising a futile paw to the glass. But mostly, they're still; for a while, I thought they were stuffed toys.

Everything should be allowed to live and die, according to its nature. But cats have two natures. Take my tortoise-shell, Melly. Indoors, she's a fawner, on to my knee the moment I sit down, purring, drooling, craving my approving hand. A harmless suppliant . . .

My neighbours call her the bird catcher. She hunts their garden, filling their empty, pensioned lives with displays of predatory cunning better than TV safaris into Africa.

She's a diplomat; never brings a bird home.

I've seen her myself, late at night, crossing the back-yards of our lane like an Olympic hurdler, under sparse orange street lamps. I've called, but she ignores me, passing overhead without a break in her stride. On the wild side.

Two natures. A purring bundle in your arms; a contemplative Buddha by the fire. But those pointed ears are moving even in sleep, listening to the windy dark outside. Suddenly, though you've heard nothing, they're on their feet, away with a thunderous rattle through the cat flap.

Sometimes they're back in your lap within five minutes; sometimes they're returned next morning (by a neighbour who can't look you in the face), a stiff-legged, sodden corpse in a plastic carrier bag. You never get a chance to say goodbye. But everything according to its nature . . .

I used to enjoy a walk on the wild side. Even into my forties, the fire only had to burn blue on a winter's night, and I was out walking under the frosty stars. But now my legs ache after a day at school; the blue-burning coals just make me fetch a whisky and snuggle deeper into my book. My cats walk the wild side for me, coming home with a hint of rain on their fur, or spears of cold, or the smell of benzine from the old chemical works. When I bury my face in their coats, I know what the world's doing outside.

Like the Three Kings, they bear gifts. Live worms, that I return instantly to the nearest patch of earth. Tattered moths, beyond saving, transformed from fun to food in one scrunch. Once my old tom, Ginger, taunted because he couldn't hunt like the girls, returned with that mournful yowl of success and a packet of fresh bacon in his mouth. I fried it for supper, gave him his tithe.

But the oddest thing Ginger brought home, on a Halloween of intense frost, was a tiny live kitten, exactly the same colour as himsef. That was the only reason we didn't think it was a rat, for its ears were still flat to its skull, its eyes unopened, and it was soaking in his mouth.

We shouted ridiculous things at him, demanding to know where he got it, insisting he take it back to its mother. He blinked his ridicule and left the house, implying he'd done his bit and it was now up to us.

My wife was a loving soul. She didn't love cats much; just all living things, and cats for my sake. Our hearth rug became an instant hospital of tumbled blankets and screwed-up towels, warm milk, and eyedroppers. She took over the fiddly business of six feeds a day.

Typically, the young female (for she was female, though ginger) repaid her efforts by becoming entirely devoted to me. From the beginning, she slept contented on my shoulder while I read. By four weeks, she would slowly and agonisingly climb my legs to get there.

I called her Rama, for no particular reason. My wife said it sounded like a brand of furniture polish. For all her poor beginning, Rama grew amazingly fast. At Christmas, in a fit of childish glee, we gave each of our cats a lump of chicken. There was a sudden spat, and when we looked again, Rama had one piece under each paw and one in her mouth. Young as she was, none of the others tried a challenge. That night, Ginger left home for good and took up residence at the village launderette.

Then came the battle for my lap, which any male owner of she-cats knows. The others would often lie side by side, apparently peaceful, but occasionally stretching and trying to push each other off. Or they'd deliberately lie on top of each other, making me part of a cat sandwich. They'd even come to blows between my legs, which is worrying if not downright agonising.

Rama had no truck with that sort of thing. The moment she entered the room, she'd give one *look*, and the occupant of my knee would instantly depart.

She had the same effortless dominance at mealtimes. Four cats jostling at one saucer, and Rama eating lazily from the other. And they'd never dare *sniff* her leavings, even after she'd left the room.

And still she grew. Bigger even than old Melly, who was big for a cat. Every morning, as I brushed my hair before school, I would watch a little comedy. Rama would sit by our front gate, willing to receive all the world. And most passers-by would come across to stroke her, for she was very beautiful with her long, swirling red fur and plumed tail. But as they drew near, and saw her great size, and felt her confidence, they would grow . . . unsure. They would hover, hands half-out, and then they would go away again, leaving her unstroked.

When she lay on me, she began to be oppressive. Her weight was just tolerable on my aching legs, but when, consumed by some catty passion, she insisted on lying on my chest with her paws round my neck, I had to strain to breathe. And she had this habit of staring into my face at

89

a distance of five centimetres. No other cat ever did that, because for cats, eye-to-eye is a challenge. But it was me that turned my eyes away; Rama had a heavy soul, as she had a heavy body.

But her delicacy made her bearable. The others have left my thighs, my shoulders, and my back a mass of tiny red scratches, with their ill-timed leaps, frantic landings, and convulsive, sleepy stretchings. I scarcely dare go swimming – people pass remarks that embarrass my wife. But Rama never put a claw into me, save once. She was a lovely cat to doze with. After a cold, hard day at school, I tend to fall asleep over the roaring fire and the six o'clock news. With Rama on my knee, I dreamed pleasant dreams I could never remember and woke without a stiff neck, set up for the evening.

Then she began to haunt our bedroom at bedtime. Here, my wife drew the line. Rama was carried swiftly downstairs and put out. She never struggled, but there was a laying back of ears that left her opinion in no doubt. Then she discovered my wife's reluctance to get up again, once warmly tucked in. So she would conceal herself early, behind the drawn bedroom curtains or almost unbreathing in the moonlit shadow of the rubber plant. Sometimes, as I undressed, I'd spot her hiding place, but that great, cool green eye would swear me to silence. Then at my wife's first snore, Rama would ghost across the carpet and purr softly up into my arms.

Then she tried to go too far and lie between my wife and me in bed. That was enough to get my wife up again, and out Rama would go.

There, for some time, the battle line stayed drawn . . .

My son Peter, too, has always lived by his nature. A Ph.D. in zoology, then the wardenship of a famous but utterly remote Scottish bird reserve. A wife not only beautiful, but also zoological, and inured to their kind of genteel poverty. Happy with a three-bedroom cottage, a chemical loo, and the use of the firm's Land-Rover.

Usually they manage things so that their babies are born in late July, when we can go up to Scotland and hold the fort. My wife copes with the children. I clumsily take

Sheila's place, putting plastic rings on ducks, cleaning oiled cormorants, stopping elderly ornithologists falling over cliffs, and being bossed around by Peter. My son is always at his most touching when about to become a father. For a few days he stops being a totally competent thirty-year-old and runs his fingers through his hair like a baffled teenager, his thin wrists sticking miles out of the sleeves of his well-darned jumper.

But this year, for all their Ph.D.s, they'd mistimed things. The baby was due in November. My wife drove herself up. There were snow warnings out, and I was quite frantic until I got her call from the reserve. Then I felt sorry for myself. Our house is large, Victorian, rather isolated on the crest of the hill above the old chemical works. In fact, the old manager's house. I'd got myself a mansion on the cheap, because the view of the works halved the price, though there's a splendid view of the Frodsham Hills beyond.

Our social life is usually too busy for my taste, on top of parents' evenings and all that nonsense without which the modern parent does not think her child is being educated. But now I learned that it was purely my wife's creation; you can't hold dinner parties without cooking. And I dislike going to the cinema on my own. In fact, I discovered that after thirty years of marriage, I disliked going *anywhere* on my own. I got pretty lonely, but I was too tired with the end of term to do anything about it.

I noticed the wind for the first time; the way the Virginia creeper tapped on the windows. My wife's presence had always abolished such things. I wasn't *scared*. More like a primitive man, exploring after dark a cave that had always been a bit too big for him and is now much too big. My eyes noticed new shadows in the hall; my ears twitched too often as I ate my lukewarm baked beans in the big, cold kitchen.

The cats were a solace. With Rama on my kness, and the others perched on a chairback and mantelpiece, we were famously snug. But only Rama came to bed with me. When I wakened in the night (which I never normally

91

do), it was good to feel her weight on the bed and to reach out and feel her large, soft, furry flank rising and falling.

So I was all the more annoyed, one windy night, to be awakened at three by her insistently scratching at the door, demanding to be let out. You didn't leave Rama scratching long, if you valued your paintwork.

'Go on, then, damn you.' She vanished like a ghost along the hall, and I went back to a cold bed, feeling thoroughly deserted.

I had just dozed off when the screaming started.

Now as a Head, I consider myself an expert on the female scream – hysterical, expectant, or distressed. I really can tell from a scream outside our house whether a young woman is merely drunk, or quarrelling with another female or being sexually assaulted, enjoyably or otherwise. In fact, by sallying forth, I have prevented at least two rapes, for the area of dirty grass and trees round the old works seems to attract far more couples than our pleasant municipal park.

But this was a man screaming, in such terror as I'd not heard since my army days. Inside my house. Downstairs.

I leaped out of bed, shaking from head to foot; my pyjamas had a distressing tendency to fall down. The screaming went on and on. A door slammed. Other voices shouting. Breaking crockery.

I dialed 999 on the bedside extension and was glad to hear the policeman's voice. When I hung up I felt braver, especially as silence had fallen. I went to Peter's old bedroom and got his .22 rifle, remembering the good times we'd had with it, harming nothing more than empty bottles floating in the old chemical sump. I found his box of cartridges and loaded with trembling fingers. Then, against my policeman's advice, I went downstairs, switching on every light as I passed.

The kitchen was appalling; chairs tossed over, a sea of broken crockery scrunching underfoot, the back door swinging. Splashes of red among the broken saucers. I thought someone had broken my bottle of tomato ketchup, but when I tasted it, it was blood.

Oh, my poor cats . . . they live in the kitchen at night.

But when I looked around, there they were – Melly and Tiddy and Vicky and Dunnings – perched high on the Welsh dresser, crouching under the gas stove, saucer-eyed, paralysed with terror, but otherwise unharmed. All except Rama, my poor Rama, who had tried to warn me only ten minutes before.

The policeman came in through the swinging back door, the radio clipped to his tunic prattling.

'You the householder, sir?'

'I phoned you, yes.'

He looked round. 'Burglary or domestic quarrel?'

I wondered how some people must live, then said shortly, 'My wife's away in Scotland. I'm alone in the house.'

'Better put that gun down, sir. Is it loaded?'

I put the safety catch on. 'I have a licence,' I said, wondering how out of date it was.

Another policeman appeared, dangled his hand knowingly through a circular hole in the glass of the back door. 'Burglary – pro job. There's a thirty-hundredweight van parked down the back lane. Liverpool registration – some punter called Moore – they're sussing him out on the crime computer now.'

'Some burglary – you seen *that*?' The first copper indicated a gout of blood with his shiny toe cap. 'You're not injured, sir?' They surveyed my sagging pyjamas.

'No, no!'

Their eyes went as hard as marbles. 'You shot someone, sir? In the course of preventing the burglary?'

'No, no. Smell the gun – it's not been fired.' They smelled it and looked even more baffled.

'I'm afraid they may have killed one of my cats,' I said. It was absurdly hard not to cry.

They noticed the cats for the first time; poked their rigid bodies.

'One missing, sir? Lot of blood for a cat . . .'

'They've left a nice set of dabs.' The second policeman pointed to the wall behind the open back door.

On it was a complete print of a human hand, made in what appeared to be blood.

*

I wearily picked up the last fragment of crockery and put it in the waste bin. Ran some water into a bucket and began to wash the floor. The forensic experts had taken till lunch-time and made the mess a hell of a sight worse. I wasn't going to make it to school that day. I'd just rung my secretary when the doorbell rang.

White raincoat, trilby hat. Sergeant Watkinson, CID.

'You'll be pleased to hear we picked up one of the gang, sir. *And* we got the names of the rest. He told us everything we wanted to know – when he came out from the anaesthetic.'

'Anaesthetic?'

'We picked him up at Liverpool City Hospital. They'd dumped him there – couldn't cope. He'd lost an eye.'

'An eye?' I said stupidly. He changed tack, keeping me guessing.

'They're a known gang, specialising in antiques. Come round the houses, asking if you've got any antiques to sell; then they break in and take them anyway, a week later. A nasty lot. I'm glad you didn't . . . encounter them, sir.'

'But what *happened*?'

'I believe you keep cats, sir?' He had a . . . hunting look on his face.

I nodded toward my still-shaken brood, still huddled around the kitchen. He reached out and stroked them tentatively, one by one. 'Not very big, are they, sir . . . as domestic cats go? I mean, they *look* harmless enough. This cat that was missing . . . it hasn't returned, has it? How big was that one?'

'Just a big domestic cat . . . what are you getting at, sergeant?'

'Well – that bloke we've caught – he reckoned he got mauled by something big in the dark. You don't keep exotic cats, do you, sir? A leopard or a cheetah? Very popular they're getting, with folk who can afford them.'

'Nothing like that. Just a large domestic cat. Of course, we do get tomcats visiting through the cat flap. A wild tom, cornered in a strange house, can get very nasty.'

'Yeah.' He didn't sound convinced. 'That bloody hand-print we found on the wall, sir – doesn't correspond to any named member of the gang – a woman's print they think – long fingernails.' He looked at me expectantly.

'I'm afraid I can't help you, sergeant. My wife keeps her fingernails short.'

'Where's your wife staying, sir – at the moment?'

I gave him my son's phone number. 'Can I wash that handprint off the wall now?'

'You can try, sir. Try a bit of biological detergent. Blood's hard to shift.'

'Anything else?'

'Give me a ring if that other cat shows up, sir. I'd like to see it.' He paused, one hand on the open front door. 'I don't see why that villain should lie, sir – he wasn't in any fit state to lie.'

'Cup of tea, sergeant?'

'If you're making one, sir.' It was the third time he'd come back in search of Rama. Without success. After a week, she was still missing. But something kept drawing him to our house. CID, too, must live by their own nature.

'Your case is all sewn up,' he said, spooning in two sugars. 'We picked up the last lad yesterday, and he admitted twenty-five other break-ins. Pushover. All the stuffing knocked out of him – like all the rest. We've recovered a fair bit of stolen property . . .' He stirred his tea again, needlessly. 'They were a hard lot. If you'd gone downstairs that night, they'd have put the boot in, left you for dead. So you ought to be grateful to whatever was in your kitchen . . .'

Again, he left the question hanging in the air.

'Look, sergeant, I've never kept a leopard or jaguar. How could I, without half the town knowing? I'm a public figure. Can't afford funny business.'

'I know, sir. We've made inquiries. Very solid gentleman you are, Mr Howard Snowdon. Member of Rotary . . . well liked, too. A bit overfond of pussies, but quite *ordinary* pussies.'

'You be careful, sergeant, or I'll start making inquiries about *you*.'

'About me, sir?'

'Your inspector is one of my old boys – so are three of your subordinates. Headmasters have their powers, too, you know.'

He grinned; I grinned. He'd been good company the last week. Which had been lonelier than ever in Rama's absence.

He stood up, and shook hands. 'Well, you've seen the last of me, sir. Case all sewn up. Except I don't know what I dare put in my official report . . . that would stand up in court. I don't like loose ends . . .'

I saw him to the gate in the dusk, waited while he started his car, waved as he drove off. Turned.

Rama was sitting on the doorstep, the light of the hall behind her. At least, a silhouetted cat sat there; a very big cat indeed.

I didn't walk directly to the front door; followed the curve of the drive, because the lawn was wet, and I was only in my carpet slippers.

If it wasn't Rama, it would run away as I approached.

If it didn't run away, it must be Rama.

The cat watched me silently, only turning its head slightly as I walked round the curve. Surely it was the light behind her that made her seem so big?

Three metres away, I faltered. Suppose it didn't run away, and it wasn't Rama?

'Rama? Rama?'

No response. There was a gardening fork, stuck in the earth of the rose bed, where I'd been turning over after pruning. Slowly, I reached out my hand. I felt much better, holding the fork.

Still the cat neither moved nor spoke.

This would never do; outfaced by a bloody alley cat? I advanced, thrusting the tines of the fork before me.

Immediately the cat stood up, stretched fore and aft luxuriously. Its plumed tail shot up in greeting, tip tilted slightly left. Prook of greeting.

Rama; almost as if she was laughing at me. I picked her up bodily and carried her in. She felt bigger; several pounds heavier. Living wild, eating fresh bloody protein. Plenty of rats in the old works; even rabbits, now it's been shut for years and the grass is growing between the cobbles.

She kneaded her paws against my chest ecstastically, extruding and withdrawing her claws. I felt them, I can tell you, right through my thick pullover. I told her to lay off, but she wouldn't. I grabbed the worst-offending paw, felt the heavy bones expanding and contracting; quite beyond my power to keep them still. It was a relief to dump her on the kitchen table.

'Where've you been, you bad girl? You've had me worried sick.'

Then I realised she hadn't really; all through her absence, the other cats hadn't dared touch her food in the second saucer or lie on my lap. They'd known she was coming back, and so, subconsciously, had I.

She extended one forepaw along the tabletop. Splayed out, a cat's paw looks like a knuckled human hand in a velvety glove, with claws where human fingernails should be. She licked between her fingers, cleaning. I looked for signs of blood, human blood.

Her paws were spotless; but then they always were.

I sat watching her eating. Recently, I'd taken to drawing the kitchen curtains at dusk, because my back garden is full of conifers as tall as a man, and when the wind got into them, they moved in a way that worried the corner of my eye. The wind was moving them tonight. There was even a white plastic bag caught in one that might have been an idiot face. But I knew it was only a bag, because Rama was sitting on my table eating. Her eye caught its movement for a moment, fascinated; then she dismissed it with a slight splaying of the ears and returned to her plate.

I thought of phoning Sergeant Watkinson; but what was there for him to see? I much preferred Rama's company to Sergeant Watkinson's. Having finished eating, she set to, dragging one damp paw over her ear. Even the prospect of rain seemed cosy. She would sleep in my bed tonight, while the rain battered my windows.

And if she asked to go downstairs urgently?

She was doing no more than a good watchdog. Okay,

97

the burglar had lost an eye. A Doberman pinscher would have torn his throat out. If watchdogs, why not watchcats?

Rama stopped washing and looked at me. In the dim kitchen, her pupils were dilated, round, like a woman's when she makes love. When that barrier of inhuman eye slits is removed, you can share souls with a cat, as well as with any human.

Rama loved me.

Still, I would show her who owned whom. I got down Ginger's old collar from the nail over the sink unit. (That was the one thing the couple at the launderette hadn't stolen; they'd had great pleasure returning it to me.) I wondered how Rama would take to a collar, as I fastened it with difficulty round her muscular neck. Some cats like them; some don't.

Rama seemed almost *too* pleased; rubbing her cheekbones against the knuckles of my hand with great affection.

It occurred to me the next evening that I must change the note inside her little collar-capsule. After all, she was called Rama, not Ginger, and as a headmaster, I value accuracy. I reached over to her and took the paper out. To my surprise, it was not the official piece supplied by the pet shop, but a roughly torn scrap, brown with age. On it was scrawled, in old-fashioned indelible pencil: I LUV U.

That was a phrase of my wife's; a standing joke between us. Whenever she left me a note on the kitchen table, asking me to turn on the oven or get in the washing, she ended it that way. A taunt to my headmasterly prissiness, I suppose.

But this was certainly not my wife's writing. An illiterate hand, yet forceful; the pencil had torn the paper in two places.

I turned the paper over. It carried the printed heading: BRITISH RAILWAYS. Not BRITISH RAIL, which is the modern version. It seemed to be part of a time sheet, for men doing shift work. Dates and times had been filled in with the same indelible pencil, but in the neat printing of some railway employee, no doubt. There was nothing more; the torn-off piece was, of necessity, very small to fit inside the capsule. As a last thought, I smelled it. Damp and mould and the faint whiff of benzine. It had come from the chemical works, I had no doubt.

Who on earth could have written it?

I had a strong suspicion it might be one of my own pupils. For the most puerile joke played on a Head is better than the best joke played on anybody else. Some of my colleagues have their phones ex-directory for that very reason. I didn't bother. I got on pretty well with my lot. Some even say hello to me in the street. When I first came, they called me 'The Abominable Snowdon', but over the years it's softened to 'Old Abby'.

Good joke to catch my cat, put a new message in her collar. But why not something spicier, like 'Old Abby's a poofter'? None of them would dare write 'I luv u' in front of his mates. A lone child, a lonely child? How would he know how my wife spelled it? And the writing was . . . odd, very odd. Someone trying to disguise his fist?

I put the note carefully inside our bone-dry spare teapot. Pity Watkinson couldn't test it for prints. But we don't carry fingerprint records of pupils, yet. Anyway, the surest way of encouraging this kind of nonsense is to take any notice of it.

I put a new name and address in Rama's collar, hoping that if they caught her again, they'd keep their tricks to the same semicivilised level. There were a lot of water-filled shafts in that works they could've thrown her down . . .

But I refused to keep her in; she must live according to her nature.

Then I carried her up to bed. She clung to me with flattering urgency.

It was nearly bedtime the following night, before I gave way to my impulse to look inside the name-capsule again.

Again, the name and address were gone. Another brown scrap in its place. I placed it edge to edge with the first; they fitted exactly, torn from the same sheet. Same indelible pencil; same jagged, savage writing.

KUM UP N C ME.

Another of my wife's phrases. Used when she has a mild dose of flu and has retired to bed before I return home. Those notes I *never* leave lying around. In our younger days, they led to some wild and joyous occasions, and I would still be embarrassed if Mrs Raven, our charlady, was to find one and ask what it was.

Who on earth could have got their hands on *that* phrase? It was uncanny, almost as if my wife was hiding somewhere in the house, playing games on me.

Except for the savagery of the writing.

Just then, as if to confirm her absence, my wife rang up to tell me I was a grandfather again. A bouncing boy (why do they always bounce?). Howard Anthony George. That pleased me; two of the names are mine. But I did warn Peter when he came on the line that the initials spelled 'hag' and did he want his son so lumbered? We settled for 'H. G. A.' in the end, which has a dignified cadence.

When I put the phone down, I felt much better. I placed both the evil-smelling notes into the teapot and wrote out my name and address for the third time.

'What's it all about, Rama?'

She gave a short, deep purr and splayed her ears in a noncommittal way that made me laugh.

I carried her up to bed again.

I LUV U. KUM.

The third quarter of the time sheet – the part with the signature: S. BALLARD, CHIEF SIGNALMAN. So, I knew where the sheet had come from. There had been railway sidings on the far side of the chemical works. There would be a signal box, where the points were worked from. I thought I knew where it stood. Rama had just come back from it, smelling of must and damp and benzine . . .

But why should I trail up there in the wind and dark? That'd make the little monkeys laugh. Be all over the school in no time, rocking the discipline-boat. Still (I looked at my watch) it was gone eleven; all the little darlings should be tucked up in bed by this time or at least stuck in front of the midnight movie.

Might as well stroll across and see what they'd been up to. Make sure it was nothing dangerous. I took down my old reefer-jacket off the kitchen door, got the lantern with the flashing red dome from the garage, made sure I had my door key, and set off. I'd left Rama eating a plate of cold fat pork, to the intent envy of the others. I think I had some idea of keeping her at home, out of harm's way. But before I'd gone twenty metres, I heard the cat flap bang behind me and felt her weight streak past me in the dark.

And I was glad of her company, walking through the works. God, it's an awful place. The old company had no money left to run it, and the local council had no money left to demolish it. The children haunt the works, walking along the narrow overhead pipes, climbing the rusted conveyors and high girders. The most dangerous parts have been screened off by chain link, but the children beat the chain link flat and go on with their deadly games. Graffiti everywhere, mingled with the old industrial notices, under the wavering beam of my lantern.

No. 5 HOIST MUFC RULE OK?
DANGER CAUSTIC SODA BAZZER AND JEFF AND BILLY.

We keep getting up petitions about it, and writing to our MP, but we're wasting our time. Even St George couldn't slay the dragon called No Money.

A bit of a moon broke through the clouds. The wind banged loose bits of corrugated iron, high up among the girders. My boot soles scrunched on the poisonous cinders. Dry dead leaves from God knows where, trapped like people in a disaster, scurried from place to place. I thought, if I have an accident here, it'll be days before they find me.

But the moon and my lantern saw me through, with a couple of frights, and I came out on to the open plain of the sidings. Picked my way across the moonlit empty rails to where I thought the signal box was.

But it wasn't. It was only some little platelayers' hut

101

with a stumpy chimney. The roof had fallen, and boys had lit a fire against the outside wall.

LFC RULES. JACK BERRY'S A SLIMER.

Inside, a mass of black soot and glinting shards of glass. Nothing had happened there for a very long time.

I was retracing my steps, feeling flat and foolish, when I saw a pale cat that could only have been Rama hurtling across the rails ahead of me. Following her with my eye, I at once saw the real signal box, standing in the black shadow of the limestone kiln. Rama streaked up the outside stair and vanished inside. I hurried across, worried.

The flat roof was intact, though most of the small-paned windows had been broken, making it hard to see inside the shadowy interior. I clumped up the outside stair, unnecessarily loudly, as if to warn someone I was coming, and pushed the door. It yielded enough to let a cat in, then resisted with a metallic clink. Shining my lantern, I saw a heavy chain and rusted padlock. Giving a grunt of exasperation, I was turning to descend when I thought I heard my name called from behind the door.

'Howard?'

It must be the wind, which was getting up. Good heavens, it was nearly midnight . . .

I'd descended two more stairs when the voice came again.

'Howard?' If you insist I describe that voice, I would say it was a woman's – low, hoarse, and . . . unpractised. Like a rusty gate creaking. But I didn't want to believe it was a voice, in that awful place. *Surely*, a trick of the wind?

While I was standing hovering, like a ninny, it came a third time, unmistakable.

'Howard, I love you.'

I wanted to run; but that works was no place to run through at night. So I went back and pushed the door angrily, so that the chain rattled. Called in my headmaster's voice, that sounded so hollow in the windy silence.

102

'Who's there? What's going on? Open the door!'

'Howard, I love you. Howard!'

'What are you doing with my cat? If this nonsense doesn't stop immediately, I shall fetch the police.'

There might have been a sigh at my stupidity; or it might have been the wind.

'Howard, help me. Fetch me clothes. I'm so *cold*.'

'Let go of my cat, or I will fetch the police.'

'Howard . . .' A yearning voice, a voice of endearment.

I ran down the steps, half in rage and half in terror. From a safe distance I stared up at the broken, multi-paned signal-box window. Tricky, because blowing moon-lit clouds were reflecting in the glass. But I could have sworn I saw a tall shape walking, among the signal-box levers.

'Let my cat go,' I bawled, 'or I'll fetch the police.'

Silence. I ran back up the steps, almost sobbing, and tried to kick the door in. There was a flash at my feet, then Rama was past me, and streaking across the tracks for home.

Well, I had saved my friend, and that was all that mattered. I followed her at top speed, and was never so glad to be through my own front door and switching on every light in the house. I made myself a hot whisky and lemon and sat drinking it till my shivering stopped. I was still shivering and drinking when the cat flap banged (not doing my nerves any good) and Rama came in quite cool and sat on the table washing inside her hindlegs. She gave me a couple of hard stares, as if to say 'What's all the fuss about?' Then indicated it was time for bed.

Even with her beside me, it was a long time before I slept.

Next afternoon, straight after school, I drove to the signal box, to inspect it by the last glimmerings of December daylight. Solid brick, with a concrete-slab roof. Many broken panes, but the wooden window frames intact. Nothing bigger than a cat could have wriggled through. The only way in was through the upstairs door. Laughing at my stupid fancies of the night before, I climbed the stair and rattled the chain. The lock was rusted solid; it would take an hour's work with a hacksaw . . .

'Howard?'

It shocked me more in daylight. God, how it shocked me. Cars were passing on the distant main road across the sidings, their headlights casting pools of sanity. But also reminding me it was getting dark again.

'Howard, *please*. I need clothes. I'm so *cold* . . .'

'Who are you? How do you know my name?'

'Howard, bring clothes . . . I need clothes.'

'How did you get in there? What d'you want clothes *for?*'

'Because I am *naked*, Howard. See!'

I put my eye to the crack of the door. Saw rough floorboards, the rusting leavers sticking up at all angles, the broken glass.

Then an eye swam out of the gloom, opposite mine. An eye I knew, yet somehow could not place.

'If you don't bring clothes, I shall come to you naked, Howard.'

I ran all the way back to my car.

I was tempted to sleep elsewhere that night. But when headmasters start staying in hotels in our town . . .

I locked the doors and snibbed the windows. Drew the curtains. Told myself to be sensible. But it's less easy to be sensible after dark, especially alone. The wind's an enemy of common sense, and the Virginia creeper tapping, and the idiot face in the back garden . . .

My wife rang up, full of good news about mother and baby. For once, I couldn't be bothered with her. Her cheerfulness irritated, like a bluebottle buzzing against a window. I got rid of her as quickly as possible, cooked an early supper, and quite failed to eat it. Finally I scraped it into the dish for the cats.

Only to discover there wasn't a cat in the kitchen. Odd! When you keep five cats there's always a couple loafing around, ear cocked for the sound of a dish being scraped.

I suddenly felt immensely lonely; damned them for

their ingratitude. Then steeled myself to open the back door and call them.

The wind snatched away my voice; none of them answered. The wild bushes tossed their heads at me. The dead leaves in the yard scurried around like the trapped crowd in a burning theatre. The sound of dead leaves is the deadest sound in the world; they sound the same at night in Pompeii.

I stepped out angrily to snatch the bobbing idiot-head bag from its bough. Lost my nerve halfway, ran back inside, and bolted the door. For a moment it shut out the noise of wind and leaves, and I heard, through the slightly open laundry door, the sound of a cat coughing. The sickening way they cough when they crouch flat to the ground and stick their necks out, so long you think they're choking to death.

A sign of fear in a cat. I followed the noise. The laundry seemed empty. The arrangement of washing machine and blue plastic bowl that I'd left myself the day before seemed to sneer at me. I was just putting the light out, thinking I'd been imagining things, when the low, desperate coughing started again.

There was a deep, dark, narrow gap between the cupboard and the wall. I thrust my hand in and felt, at the back, a wire-tense bundle of fur, which I dragged out by the scruff. She fought all the way, digging in her claws and ripping the lino. Melly. For a second she lay still in my arms, eyes screwed tight-shut, ears back. Then she exploded back into the narrow gap like a furry missile, knocking over a chair that stood in her way. Leaving me with a torn shirt and bleeding arms.

I left her; I know terror when I see it. Perhaps she'd had a near miss with a car . . . By morning, she'd be herself again.

I was getting a whisky when it occurred to me there might be other cats hiding in the house. A careful search revealed the three little ones in the back of my tool cupboard, a huddle of mindless terror, quite impervious to the sharp edges on the saws and chisels they were crouching on.

They couldn't all have had near misses. Something was terrifying them. It made the bolted doors and curtained windows seem pretty thin. I wished Rama was here. Rama wouldn't frighten so easy. But of Rama there was no sign, even in the draughty attics.

I had an absurd desire to call Sergeant Watkinson. But what about? It was gone eleven, and the world was away, asleep. It wouldn't want to know about my problems, at least till morning. Self-help, Howard, self-help! I went up to Peter's room to get the rifle. Again, the oily smell of cartridges reminded me of happier days. Would they still work, after ten years? Though God knew what I intended to shoot that night. Only *I* wasn't giving up my eyes without a struggle.

I made up a big fire in the lounge; pushed furniture against the windows, with some absurd idea of tripping up anything that tried to come through them. Settled in my armchair with another, very small whisky. Didn't want my wits fuddled. I tried playing some Bach on the record-player; but the sound blocked out all other noises and I switched off quickly again. I finally settled with the gun across my knee, the lantern beside me in case the lights went out, and *The Lord of the Rings* balanced across the gun. But Frodo's journey – my favourite passage in all literature – was no comfort. I was listening, listening, checking each noise as it came. A hunted animal in its lair, but at least an animal with some teeth.

But we're not as good as animals at staying alert. Whether it was the whisky or the fire, I began to doze. Twice, the book falling from my lap brought me leaping awake. Once, it was the collapse of coals in the fire. Once, the grandfather clock in the hall, chiming one, sounding as meaningless as it would to a cat.

And yet, in the end, my senses did not let me down. Suddenly, I came out of sleep wide-awake, not knowing what had wakened me. But I somehow knew this was it. I remember putting my book and whisky glass carefully on one side, out of harm's way; picking up the gun and pointing it at the white door of my lounge, and not forgetting to slip off the safety catch.

At the back of the house, the cat flap banged. Which of

the little cats was moving? Or had Rama come home? I wasn't tempted to go and look; just kept sitting in my chair, pointing the rifle with fairly steady hands.

I never heard any footsteps; just the floorboards in the hall, creaking. Something heavier than a cat.

The door handle rattled three times, as a cat will sometimes rattle it, wanting to be in. The third time, it began to turn, hesitantly, as if the creature wasn't used to opening doors. I had an awful temptation to shoot through the white door, just above the handle, to hear a heavy body fall and know that I was safe. To kill what stood there, without having to look at it. But I'm a man, not an animal.

The door opened only five centimetres; a five-centimetre gap of darkness, and something taking stock of me, out of that darkness. I nudged up the barrel of the gun, to warn whatever stood there not to try my patience too long.

'Howard?' It was the voice from the signal box.

At that moment, I realised I was still wearing my reading spectacles, and everything more than a metre away was a blur. My outdoor spectacles were on the table beside me, but to reach them, I'd have to take one hand off the gun.

The door swung open, and I thought I was going crazy.

Mrs Raven stood there in the shadows; Mrs Raven, our cleaner, in her big-checked nylon overall.

'Mrs Raven,' I said, dumbfounded. 'What are *you* doing here?' I remember thinking, ridiculously, that this was Monday night – well, Tuesday morning – and Mrs Raven came on Thursdays. Then the creature swam in from the shadows, and even wearing my reading spectacles, I realised I wasn't talking to Mrs Raven, but something dressed in Mrs Raven's overall. That always hung on the back door, above the cat flap.

Where Mrs Raven's headscarf usually hid her curlers flamed a mane of burning red hair. Where Mrs Raven's wrinkled grey stockings covered a pair of spindleshanks . . . the overall, which enclosed Mrs Raven like a voluminous sack, was no more than a minidress on this thing.

107

She flowed in like a wave of grace, filling the room. She'd have flowed right over me, but I raised the small, mean barrel of the gun.

That stopped her; whatever she was, she knew what a gun was for.

She curled herself smoothly down into my wife's chair, across the fireside. Without human modesty; so I was glad I was wearing my reading spectacles. All her body hair seemed that same flaming red. She made my wife's chair look small; she made the room feel small; and it's not a small room. I wondered again about changing my spectacles, but she'd be across the hearth rug in a flash if I took my eyes off her.

'Howard?'

I peered. Got a blurred impression of large green eyes and, when she yawned, very white teeth. She was no more humanly modest with her yawn than with her body. Just yawned enjoyably to the fullest extent, without putting her hand over her mouth.

'You do know me, Howard.' She tried to stretch again; but the nylon overall was a constricting torment to her. She put up a hand and the nylon ripped open, as if it were paper. From the sound, I could imagine the size of her fingernails.

'You remind me . . . of my cat Rama,' I said, forcing a laugh; not wanting to be totally outfaced. It seemed a good, brave thing to laugh at such a monster.

'I *am* your cat Rama.'

Then I knew I was asleep and dreaming. The dreams of a lonely fifty-year-old, whose wife has been away too long. But a man must act in his dreams as he would act in life. Or else he is a hypocrite. So I kept the dream gun pointing at her.

'If you are my cat Rama, you will behave like my cat Rama. At least while you are in *my* house. What you do outside is your own business.'

I jumped awake to the rattle of the cat flap, to find I was in a cold and empty room. No wonder the room was so cold; the draught had swung the door open five centimetres . . .

*

108

I didn't stir from my chair for the rest of the night, though I made the fire up several times and dozed till daylight. Some dreams can leave a heavier impression on you than reality. I wakened finally with bright early sunshine making streaks across the darkened hearth rug. I pulled back the curtains, feeling a total fool, with a very stiff neck as a memento of my foolishness. The book, the gun, and the whisky glass were not a welcome sight.

I checked the house; every door and window was, of course, locked and secure. My five cats gave me their usual sleepy, stretching greeting when I entered the kitchen. I had to stroke their heads in turn; Rama first, of course. I tried staring her out and failed as usual. Otherwise she seemed perfectly normal. I felt a certain reluctance to touch her at all but made myself. I am not the kind of person who blames a cat for my own silly dreams. Nevertheless, from that day there was a coldness, a distance between us.

Mrs Raven's overall hung on the door as usual. Except that when I turned it around, all the buttons were missing and seemed to have been removed with unnecessary force. I found them in the pocket. That seemed a little odd, but then I'd never taken any interest in the garment before. Perhaps my wife or Mrs Raven was busily engaged in taking it in, or letting it out, or some other mysterious thing that women seem always to be doing to garments. Certainly the overall wasn't seriously damaged. Nothing Mrs Raven couldn't put right in ten minutes. I made a resolve to ask her about it but forgot and never did.

Life continued much as before, except that Rama seemed to get ever bigger and sleeker. And I felt an increasing reluctance to join my family in Scotland for Christmas and leave Mrs Raven and Rama to each other's tender mercies.

But Christmas was still ten days off when it happened. I was buying my supper in the village off licence, when I heard about it. A young girl, on her way home alone from a Christmas dance the previous night, had been dragged into the old works and murdered.

'I saw the young copper who found her,' said the

woman behind the counter, her eyes wide upon the horror of some inward scene. 'I had to give him a cup of tea, he was that shaken. He was sick all over the bathroom floor. He said it was like a wild beast had mauled her to death . . .'

I just stood there, with my cold Cornish pasties in my hand, afraid I was going to drop them. I remember that there was a young man standing opposite me in the queue. A small young man in a black leather jacket, a workman of some kind, because he had a bag of tools in his hand, with the handle of a hammer and the point of a screwdriver sticking out. He kept staring at the woman and then staring at me, drinking in our faces, and I remember thinking he knows something, he knows about me and about Rama. I heard no more; I was only too eager to get out of the shop without disgracing myself.

When I got home, Rama was nowhere to be seen. Sergeant Watkinson rang the bell, as I was sitting in the cold kitchen, staring blankly at the pages of an old colour supplement.

I couldn't help glancing at Rama's usual chair as I showed him in.

'Something missing, sir?'

'No, no,' I said, elaborately counting the four cats that remained. 'Four – all accounted for.'

'The other one never turned up, then?'

I shook my head. He'd never believe any of it, anyway. Besides, this was between me and Rama.

He asked if I'd heard anything the previous night. Living in the house nearest the old works . . . I shook my head with conviction. That much was true. I asked about the girl's injuries. He just shook his head. Nothing was being released.

When he'd gone, I went to Peter's room and took down the rifle.

The next week was hell. The gun was always ready, but there was no sign of her. The other cats began to eat her food, sleep in her chair. I don't know how I got through school. In the evenings, I drank. My wife sensed my

110

mood over the phone; threatened to come home. I managed to put her off.

Then, the night before the end of term, I looked up at the uncurtained window (I no longer bothered to draw the curtains) and saw her great cat-mask peering at me. I wasn't frightened; only in despair that she would vanish like a ghost before I could fetch the gun.

But when I returned she was still there, staring in calmly, sadly – almost, I would have said, lovingly. I fumbled with the safety catch, raised the rifle to shoot her through the glass, and her head immediately vanished.

I ran outside into a clear moonlit night. She stood on top of the yard gate, silvered by the moon. I raised the rifle, and again she dropped out of sight.

I ran after her, like a mad thing, in my shirtsleeves. Saw her streaking down the grass slopes to the old works, far ahead, too difficult a shot by moonlight. I ran without hope, then. She would lose me in the works, easily; be crouched on a girder, above my head, and I'd never notice.

But when I reached the works she was visible, a pale streak trotting along the main soda pipe. I began to suspect she was playing with me, as if I was a mouse. Leading me to what? Her death? My death? I no longer cared. My middle-aged breath scraped harshly in my throat, tasting foully of whisky and despair.

Half an hour later, on the slope of Brinkton Woods, I knew she was leading me on. Letting me draw nearer and nearer, yet always on the move; never giving me the chance of a straight shot.

Then, in the depth of the wood, she vanished. I sat on a fallen tree, sweating and gasping and wishing I was dead. Brinkton Woods is for lovers, not cats and crazy, middle-aged men. I felt too weak to walk two miles home. Why had she *done* this to me? I didn't care if she killed me.

So why did I start up in fright at a crashing in the nearby bushes? It didn't sound like Rama anyway; much too noisy and disorganised.

Then a young girl screamed.

111

An ugly sound; a thud on flesh. Then the scream turned into a sobbing, a wild sobbing of sheer disbelief.

'Oh, no, oh, no, oh, no, please don't, please don't.'

Another ugly noise, before it got into my thick skull that the girl might be being murdered. I'd never heard the sound of a killing before; it doesn't sound like you expect it to sound, from the telly.

I slipped off the safety catch and ran. Oh, Rama!

I burst through the bushes into a tiny clearing where the moonlight lay full. A girl lay on her back, skirt up round her waist, pale, silken legs thrashing wildly while something dark crouched with horrible intentness over her head and neck.

As I raised my rifle, uncertain of getting in a shot, wondering whether to leap in and use it like a club, the girl gave one last, desperate, upward push with her bleeding arms. Just for a second, the dark shape hung abover her, quite separate . . .

I fired at the centre of the rib cage. No animal can do much harm once you've hit it in the rib cage, even if you don't find the heart.

I was too close to miss, even by moonlight. The beast fell sideways, pivoting on the girl's outstretched arms, and lay quite still.

'Goodbye, Rama,' I mouthed bitterly, and walked across. The girl mustn't have been hurt too badly. She had leaped to her feet and began screaming again for all she was worth. Perhaps she thought I was the second murderer.

The beast had rolled into the shadow of a bush. I pushed it with my foot, still covering it with the rifle.

It was a man.

A small, dark man in a black leather jacket. A bag of tools lay beside him – hammer and screwdriver. He was quite dead; a small, damp, warm patch where his heart would be.

A feeling of being watched made me look up. Rising above the bush was a head, with two great, dark, sorrowful eyes and a mane of hair that managed to look red even in the moonlight.

Rama raised one hand.

'Goodbye, Howard.' It had sadness and longing and contempt in it.

Then Rama was gone, forever.

GOLIATH

When I was ten, we went to live in Countess Sikorski's pie factory. We had to. We were poor; my father was an artist, but nobody liked his paintings then. My mother kept us. She was a potter, and loved to make tall beautiful pots, but she never got the chance. Instead, she had to make little ashtrays at five pounds the dozen. With little birds painted on them, and 'A present from Bridport'. I can see her now, straightening up from the long rows of ashtrays, driving both hands into the small of her back to ease the pain, and staring blankly into space. Thinking there *must* be more to life than ashtrays. But she loved my father, so she kept going.

Mind you, as pie factories go, ours wasn't bad. Don't imagine tall smoking chimneys and miles of grey streets. We lived in the pretty village of Appledown, and the pie factory was a Georgian double-fronted house, though a bit battered and leaky. In front was a cobbled yard, and on each side of the yard were buildings: a coachhouse and stables. In the old stables, my mother made her ashtrays; in the hayloft above, my father painted. And across the yard, in the old coachhouse, the Countess Sikorski made her famous pies, on a long row of gas cookers, some of which must have dated back to Queen Victoria, if not Boadicea. She got the village women in to help, and at the end of a morning, when the huge table in the middle was filled with pies of every size, they would stand in the door of the coachhouse fanning themselves, and wiping the sweat off their red faces with their discarded aprons.

The Countess Sikorski should've been popular; she brought work to the village; she made wonderful pies. Her pies were famous throughout the county, and even today, forty years later, old men will still say a pie is

114

'nearly as good as a countess pie'. In her endless search for meat for them, she was the ally of every dishonest smallholder, poacher and black-market butcher for miles around, though she was never arrested for her underhand dealings. People said the Chief Constable was too fond of a countess pie, himself . . .

But she could never forget she had been a countess back in Poland before the war, and she never let anybody else forget either. Her husband the count, who had been a colonel in the Polish cavalry in 1939, and a mere lieutenant with the Free Polish Army in 1945, never mentioned it. She had demoted him very much to the rank of private, and he just drove the van that delivered the pies, and as a sideline took illegal bets for bookmakers. He was often arrested for this, but when he came up in court his shy smile, balding head and war record always got him off with a small fine. But when he got home there would always be a screaming row, and the countess would throw old boots and plates at him, and scream that he was dragging the honour of Poland through the dirt. The rows sometimes lasted all night. I got a bit tired of the honour of Poland, though I always enjoyed the thumps and crashes.

The worst thing about living in our half of the pie factory was that it was embarrassing. The countess wasn't one to miss a trick. She had a notice by the gate as big as a billboard.

FRESH PIES FOR SALE. APPLY WITHIN.
COUNTESS SIKORSKI PROPRIETRESS.

People stopped to look, in those hungry days of 1946, and the marvellous smell of pies did the rest. But the kids at school cracked jokes. They said the countess put slugs in her pies, and adders, and dead lambs and crows. They said I'd better watch out for our ginger tomcat, or he might vanish one night. In vain I protested she wasn't like that. She loved our cat; she was always giving him titbits. The other kids said she was just fattening him up . . .

To me, the countess was a fabulous monster. Nearly six

foot tall, built as broad as a statue, with a big nose and raven-black hair pulled back in a bun. She was always slipping me one of the smaller pies, while they were still hot, telling me I was too thin and small for my age, and unless I ate the pie quick, I would die of starvation, like so many Polish children had died. She had no children herself; or at least she never spoke of them.

But in return for the pie, I had to stand for hours and listen to her tale of woe; how she was cheated by dishonest poachers (I never dared ask what an honest poacher might look like), thieving farmers, and restaurant-owners who would not pay what they owed her. She would say, 'Back in Poland, in the old days, I could have that man whipped or shot like . . . pouf!' And she would reach out towards my nose, crack her great floury finger against her great floury thumb. I didn't mind listening to her; indeed I felt it was my family duty, for otherwise she would cross the yard and go on at my mother instead, as my mother stood swaying wearily, smiling blankly, across her rows of unfinished ashtrays. (My father, wise man, always stayed hidden in the hayloft with his paintings.)

I suppose she was the devil I knew. The devil I didn't – the other monster of my infant life – was Captain Cholmondely-Bottomley, the Master of the Hunt. Now the kids at school laughed at him as well. For 'Cholmondely' is pronounced 'Chumley' so the kids worked out that 'Bottomley' must be pronounced '*Bum*-ly'. So they always called him 'Chumly-*Bum*ly' and galloped across the playground jerking their bottoms in the air, in imitation of his riding style, which reduced everyone to howls of laughter.

But although Chumly-Bumly might be a big joke in the playground, outside he was very far from a joke. For the hunt terrified me. First there were the hounds. I met them on the first day I was in the village. My father had sent me for a pint of milk up to Higgin's Farm, and I met them being taken for a walk, in the narrow lane. The huntsman must have been close behind, but I couldn't see him. All I saw was this massive wave of big white, black and brown dogs running towards me – filling the tree-shadowed lane, flowing over every obstacle, blotting

116

out everything. Tongues lolling, big teeth showing, and *all* exactly the same. The same awful hunting sniffing expression, like they would eat anything they met, and the awful feeling they didn't have separate minds like ordinary dogs, but hundreds of bodies and only one mind between them.

They didn't touch me; they only sniffed and licked at me, but by the time the huntsman came into view, I was *screaming*.

Toddy Tyndale, the huntsman was very good with me; he took me home and explained. Later, he called for me and took me to the kennels to see the hounds being fed. But it didn't make me love the hounds any more. They peed on each other, as they ate; and I was still convinced they only had one dreadful mind that ruled all their bodies.

My father didn't help. He was the kindest man under the sun. A life-long Quaker, a pacifist who had served with the Friends Ambulance Unit in Finland during the war. A man who would literally not hurt a fly; who would get up from his painting and spend half an hour catching a wasp buzzing on the window, so he could release it to freedom. But we were out for a walk one winter morning, when the mist lay low on the ground, and we heard that strange cold haunting note of the huntsman's horn, and they came galloping through the mist, like something out of a nightmare.

My father's hands clenched and he said, almost to himself, 'Who do they think they *are*? I know how the archers must have felt at Crecy.' I didn't ask him about the archers at Crecy; his face was too pale and set. But I asked the teacher at school, and he told me that Crecy was a battle against the French, when the English archers killed the French horsemen to the last man and horse, so that they lay piled ten feet deep on the battlefield.

And every time the haunting note came, on a frosty morning, my father would run downstairs shouting, 'Where's the cat? Where's the cat?' And there would be a terrible panic until the cat was found, and locked in the hayloft where my father could see him. For my father said

117

the hounds tore apart any cats they found, and our cat was red, like a fox . . .

But Chumly-Bumly himself was worst of all. Another morning, I met him riding at the head of the hunt, and he pointed his riding crop at me, and then at a gate he wanted opening. He didn't say a thing, high on his great horse, just pointed. And after I had opened the gate, silent, terrified, he didn't say anything either, just galloped off. But it was the look on his face. My parents had always looked at me with smiles; so did most people. But I had known kids look at me with hate, before a fight at school, and that *hate* wasn't as bad as the look on Chumly-Bumly's face. He had a thin face, like a hatchet, and his eyes were close together, and the coldest blue I've ever seen. They made me into nothing, as if I was a thing like a fence post, or *less* than a fence post.

My mother said she supposed we had to have the hunt, to keep the foxes down to save the chickens from being eaten. Certainly there were a lot of foxes. Mainly round the countess's dustbins, in the cobbled yard. For they contained everything that did not go in the pies. That is how our cat finally got a name. For our cat knew all about the dustbins too. When he came to the pie factory he was long but thin, and had no name. We just called him 'the cat'. Then he started the battle of the dustbins with the foxes. And he filled out and finally got a name.

I used to watch him eating there with bated breath, for often the foxes came while there was still some light in the sky.

Now, nobody agrees about cats and foxes. A lot of people say foxes kill and eat all cats. And cats' skeletons, Toddy Tyndale told me, had been found in foxes' earths, when they dug them out. But there are inexperienced half-grown kittens, and foxes do get them. And there are old cats, and sick starving cats, and foxes do get them. But a full-grown tomcat, with all his wits about him? That's a different matter, I can tell you. Because I've watched. Foxes are smaller than most people think. They're not big wild dogs. They're not much bigger than a full-grown cat, and they hunt and pounce like cats, and live on mice and rats just like cats. They even move like cats, and bat their ears like cats. They're like cats with snouts. And when a cat and a fox meet, they threaten each other and make bullying moves, just like two cats do.

And usually, round our dustbins, the foxes gave way first; and hung about shiftily, at a distance, waiting for our cat to eat his fill. (Usually after the fox had had the bother of knocking the lid off, too.)

Until one evening. Our cat was just finishing his supper at the bins, when, quick as light, this fox comes out from behind the wall, and makes a rush at our cat. It was a big fox and it meant to kill and eat our cat. I could tell. I was terrified; I couldn't move or even shout from my window. But it all seemed to happen in slow motion, somehow, so I remember everything.

Our cat saw him just in time. Turned to run. And that would have been fatal. The fox would have bitten him in the neck and that would've been that. But our cat seemed to know that. Quick as light, he changed his mind and got in the gap between two bins, facing outwards. Into the gap went the fox, and out of that gap came a ginger paw full of claws. He hit the fox on the soft bit on the end of his nose, just like Jack Kramer used to hit a tennis ball at Wimbledon. Four times, quick as light. The fox stopped trying to get into the gap, and hastily backed out. He turned and looked round, and I saw the blood on the end of his nose.

But he was a tough old fox, not used to being beaten. He tried again. This time he leapt high in the air, and tried to land on our cat's back.

But before he landed, our cat had rolled over, and had all four sets of claws going like windmills. That fox got what any other tomcat would've got. And he lost his taste for it, as his fur came blowing across the cobbles in the last of the sunset, like red autumn leaves.

He backed off a couple of metres. He and our cat said certain unprintable things to each other. Then the fox turned away in despair . . .

And our cat was after him. Hit him in the middle of the back with all four paws . . .

It was nearly the end of our cat, out there in the open. There was a terrible tangle of red and ginger fur for what seemed forever . . . then they both turned their backs and walked away. As if they'd agreed it was a draw. They were both limping badly.

I ran out and picked up our cat. He was bleeding in half a dozen places (but so was the fox). Then I heard a voice say, 'He is a *hero*! He is like the Polish cavalry charging Nazi tanks in front of Warsaw, with only the banner of the Virgin to protect them! He is a real *Polish* cat!'

I looked up, and there was the countess, beaming at us both, her large dark eyes shining with the unholy light of battle.

'He is a *hero*,' she repeated. 'We shall call him *Goliath*.'

I just stood there, trembling. I thought Goliath was not a Quaker's cat. He had seen death coming for him, and had not turned the other cheek. He had turned four terrible sets of claws, and lived, bleeding, to tell the tale.

If he had turned the other cheek, he would by now be being eaten by the fox, in some hole in the earth.

It seemed a lesson worth remembering. But when my father and mother came out, full of loving concern, and took Goliath off to the vet for treatment they couldn't really afford, I just couldn't look them in the face.

Their Quaker way was wrong. *Their* Quaker way, Goliath would be dead.

Goliath's way, the countess's way, Goliath was alive.

I went to bed in a great muddle. But Goliath healed, and became true king of the dustbins, huge and unchallenged. I never saw the big fox again. I often wondered how he had managed, with no vet to look after *him*.

I remember it was a sunny morning, nearly lunch-time, when we heard the hunting horn, not far off across the fields. My father had come down into the yard to play with me, because he had just sold two pictures, and finished another, and he was pleased with himself, and felt he could waste a bit of time on fun, for once. We were playing a game of our own, with a soft tennis ball and an old baseball bat, that some Yank soldiers had left behind when they left our house after the war. My father threw the ball to me, and I had to hit it to where he *could* catch it. If he failed to catch it three times in a row, I was out. It is a game that only works when played by people who are good friends . . .

It must have been nearly twelve, because the countess had finished her morning's baking, and the air was full of the delicious smell of pies, and the village women were standing in the doorway of the coachhouse kitchen, watching us idly and fanning themselves with their aprons held loose in their hands.

The sound of the horn grew nearer.

My father said, 'Where's Goliath?' His face went as white as a sheet. We ran about the yard, calling for him, looking for him. But he was nowhere to be found. The village women started to join us in hunting and calling; they too knew what the horn meant, and they were all fond of Goliath. But they had no more luck than we did.

The sound of the horn came nearer, while we all stood silent, fidgeting. Then nearer still.

'They'm terrible close to the village,' said one of the women. 'Don't normally come this close.'

The horn again, almost at the end of the village street. Then the hounds making their noise, that terrible brain-less sound that means death to any living creature they catch.

And then they came into sight, sweeping up the narrow street, with a small thing fleeing in front of them for dear life.

'That ain't no fox,' said one of the women. 'It's ginger.'

We watched transfixed, as Goliath headed for home with death at his heels. His pride was gone, his beauty. His head was down, his tail was down as he ran blind, without hope.

But he made it to the gate, swept through my legs, and crashed head-on into the corner between the house and the bakery, a heaving collapsed bundle of fur.

And then the hounds swept into the yard.

I did not think. I just found myself standing in that corner over the exhausted body of Goliath. And I still had that big baseball bat in my hand. And the faces of the hounds, the open mouths . . .

I lashed out with the baseball bat. Again and again and again. And I was hitting hounds. I heard my father shout, my mother and the women scream . . .

Something leapt on my back, clawing and gouging me all the way up. Something leapt from my shoulder, clean over the heads of the pack. I will remember the kick of that great leap till my dying day; it nearly knocked me flat.

Goliath landed on clear cobbles. Before the hounds had more than half-turned on him, he leapt again. Straight through the open door of the bakery, straight into the middle of the tableful of steaming pies.

Yet such was his aim, that he landed in a tiny space between two of the bigger pies; he did not disturb a single one.

Then he leapt again, upwards this time, to the great narrow beam that ran across the roof of the coachhouse; caught it with his front paws, and dangled helpless there for a heart-stopping moment; until he managed to haul himself up on to the narrow beam like a very old man.

Then, gathering his tattered dignity, he turned with all four feet very close together, and spat his disdain and defiance at the pack.

As one, they leapt on to the table in pursuit. There was the amazing sight of pies and pieces of pie flying in all directions.

It finished with the utter disarray of the pack; some leapt unavailingly at the rafter, over and over again, though it was far beyond their reach. Their rebounding feet crushed the pies to pulp. Others, hungry after a morning's hunting, fell avidly to eating the best pies ever baked in the county.

Toddy Tyndale arrived, and could do nothing with them.

Chumly-Bumly arrived, and leapt from his horse, effing and blinding, and laying about him with his whip.

The countess arrived, took one look at her shattered pies, and grabbed the big yard-broom . . .

Tom Tree arrived last. He had been the wise village bobby for many years, but the situation was too much even for him.

Mind you, the hounds, weary and full of pie, had lost all taste for the chase. They let the women shoo them out into the lane, with shouts of 'Get away, you great dirty things' because some of them had cocked their legs in the bakery.

Toddy Tyndale began getting them whipped-in to go back to the kennels, but he made a slow job of it. Curiously, he kept doubling up against the wall, his back heaving strangely. Then he would throw a furtive glance at Chumly-Bumly.

But Chumly-Bumly had troubles enough of his own. Under the countess' assault with the broom, his hunting cap was gone, his hunting pink was caked with mud from his being knocked flat on to the cobbles and he had a blueing lump on his narrow forehead the size of half an egg. But he was still far too much of an English gentleman to consider offering violence to a lady, even in self-defence.

It was Tom Tree who finally got the yard-broom off the countess.

'Why haff you taken my broom? It is *my* broom, I haff paid good money for it. In England, do policemen haff the right to steal brooms? Is that a free democracy? What haff we been fighting the Nazis for, if you can steal my broom?'

'*Madam*,' said Tom Tree, as soothingly as possible.

'I insist you arrest this criminal lunatic,' she said, pointing a quivering finger at Chumly-Bumly. 'He kills harmless pets! He sets his dogs on little children! He has stolen pies to the total value of seventeen pounds, nine-teen and sixpence, retail!'

How she managed to work out the exact price while busy belabouring Chumly-Bumly, I shall never know. She added, 'In the old days, in Poland, I would have this man *whipped*. I would have him *shot*. Why do you English let

123

your criminals run wild, destroying the pies of honest women?'

'I will pay for the pies,' said Chumly-Bumly, stiffly.

'So,' said the countess, holding an outstretched quivering hand under his nose.'Where is your money?'

Of course, Chumly-Bumly had no money on him, in his hunting pink. Neither did any of the other members of the Hunt, who were watching on horseback, from a safe distance down the lane, this most un-English of spectacles.

'So. You say you will pay, but you have no money. That is fraud. Arrest this criminal lunatic for fraud, constable! I *insist*!'

Tom Tree could only shake his head like a baffled bull. After all, Chumly-Bumly *was* chairman of the local magistrates . . .

'Very well, I confiscate this horse, till the debt is paid.' And the countess began to lead away Chumly-Bumly's bay hunter . . .

I'm afraid my mother took me away at that point. It wasn't until she got me up to the bathrom that I realised my arms were bitten and bleeding in three places. She washed the wounds and put me to bed, and sent for the doctor. By that time I was trembling all over, and quite unable to lie still.

But then Goliath strolled in, sat on my bed and began to wash himself. He seemed much less upset than me. After a thorough wash, he curled up and went to sleep. I lay and listened to the countess, standing at the gate, telling all and sundry who passed about the Battle of the Pie Factory.

I heard Toddy Tyndall come with the money for the pies, and take away the horse. I heard the Countess shout after him, 'I advise you to get a new employer. *I* would not work for a pie-thief!'

I didn't hear what Toddy said in reply; the doctor had just come, and he gave me two injections, that hurt quite a lot.

But not as much as my father's face, when I saw it.

He sat on my bed and said slowly, 'You broke a hound's jaw . . .' But it was more than the jaw, which would heal.

He had seen me choose to fight. He had seen me use violence. He didn't have to say anything; it was all on his face. We sat silent a long time. Then he said, 'Violence never solved anything, son.'

I couldn't say anything back.

I just reached out and stroked Goliath's warm, purring mass.

My father and I looked at each other, silently. We knew. He had chosen his way, and I had chosen mine.

It was never quite the same, afterwards.

THE CAT, SPARTAN

I was almost happy at Granda's funeral. It was his own church, see? Where he took the collection and counted it in the vestry afterwards, and let me help when I was little. Where he rang the bells and mowed the churchyard.

His mate the vicar told us what a good old boy he'd been, who would do anything for anybody. And the church was full of flowers from the village gardens, glowing against the grey stone. All except the awful wreath of lilies my parents had sent from the florists in town.

And afterwards, at the church door, the whole village must've come and shaken me by the hand, and everybody said what a good old boy he'd been.

And Spartan was there all the time. He came in last, walking up the aisle as slow and solemn as a judge, and sat by the coffin right through the service. And the village people nodded, and gave each other fleeting funeral smiles.

And Spartan followed the coffin to the grave, which was on the warm south side of the churchyard. The place Granda had chosen, near the big yew that's been there since Cromwell's time. And Spartan followed us with his eyes, as we each sprinkled soil on the coffin in the grave with a sandy rattle.

I just couldn't believe that Granda was down there in the horrible shiny dark coffin, with its vulgar shiny brass handles. He wasn't fastened up in there; he was *everywhere* now. Watching over his church and his friends round the grave, the sunlit trees and the cornfields all round. Watching, and pleased. Especially with Spartan.

We left Spartan carefully supervising the gravediggers filling in the grave, and straggled down towards the gate.

And then it went all wrong.

Batty Henty was talking to me, tears in his eyes, holding both my hands. He's not at all batty really, even if he does live alone, and can't read or write. He can tell tomorrow's weather, and he's never wrong. Any animal will come to him.

Batty was telling me what they *all* thought, 'Yer Granda shoulda lain in his own house, where he belonged to be. Not in that there undertakers . . .' when my father came up tight-lipped and said we had to be going. He ignored Batty like he was the gatepost.

So we left in the Merc; and the village people followed us with their eyes, and did not wave. They knew we'd done wrong, not giving Granda a proper send-off after the funeral, back at his cottage. With ham sandwiches and a drop to drink, and lots of stories, like the hare that jumped over Granda's head in the harvest field . . .

On the way to the solicitor's my mother said, 'How soon can we get his cottage on the market? People go off buying houses in winter.'

My father said, 'Oh, I don't know. The way house prices are rising, it might pay to hang on till spring . . .'

'And risk squatters?'   .

'It's not an area for squatters.'

'But . . . what about all Granda's *things*?' I said. 'What about Spartan?' It came out as a kind of feeble squeak from the back seat. I knew it was no good, before I said it.

'Whately's have offered most for the house clearance,' said my mother. 'And I've rung the RSPCA to come and deal with Spartan.'

I might as well not have existed.

Granda might as well not have existed.

Soon Spartan would cease to exist. My mother was efficient. She already had the date of Granda's death in her filofax, so she could phone the papers to insert anniversary memories next year.

God, Granda, where *are* you? Why did you have to go and get yourself killed? And leave me with these two . . . *vultures*? What can I *do*? If I make a fuss, they'll call it

127

teenage tantrums. If I make a big enough fuss, they'll probably send me to a shrink.

Granda's voice inside my head. 'Patience, our Tim. Slow and steady wins the race!' But it was only a memory. What can a memory do against *vultures*?

'Can we hurry it along, Mr Makepeace?' asked my father. 'I have another appointment at four.'

Appointment? Playing squash with John Victor. Of Victor Enterprises PLC. A *very* important business client. And my mother would be itching to start chopping and blending in her wonderful fitted kitchen, because the horrible Southwarks were coming to dinner.

Mr Makepeace looked up over his half-spectacles. Tapped Granda's will with the nail of his forefinger. He was an old mate of Granda's. They used to go shooting pigeons together. Mr Makepeace should've looked sad. But he looked like a little boy about to light a firework. Was *nobody* sad about Granda?

Then he straightened his face, as became a family lawyer.

'I'm afraid this will come as rather a shock . . .'

'Shock?' said my mother, very hard and quick. 'What kind of shock?'

Mr Makepeace was quietly enjoying himself. Kept on tapping the will, like he was Jimmy Connors about to serve an ace. Like he was a terrorist loading his gun.

'Everything has been left to the grandson.' He nodded at me.

'The bloody old *fool*,' said my father, savagely.

'We'll see about *that*,' said my mother.

'The will is quite valid,' said Mr Makepeace. 'He was of sound mind and testamentary disposition. It's not unusual for everything to be left to a *beloved* grandchild.'

'He's not old enough,' said my mother, as if she was swatting a bluebottle that had dared to enter her beloved fitted kitchen. 'He can't be expected to take on such responsibilities.'

'Surely we must hold it in trust for him?' said my father.

'The boy is, I think, eighteen?' said Mr Makepeace.

128

'This is ridiculous,' said my mother. 'There *must* be a way . . .'

'No way,' said Mr Makepeace, 'to dispossess your own son. The will is very frank. It gives reasons. Would you want those reasons made public?'

My mother flinched. Alpotton's a small town; people gossip. Clients might get to hear; very bad for business.

My parents turned and looked at me. You know that look? The start of World War Three? I hope for your sake you don't. My parents knew they couldn't shake Makepeace. So they were about to start on me. All the way home in the car. All the rest of my life, till I gave in. They might even cancel a few appointments, so they could go on chewing me over. Even John Victor. Even the horrible Southwarks . . .

'I should like a little time alone with the heir, now, please,' said Mr Makepeace. He really loved himself saying that.

So did I.

My parents blundered out. Like the Wicked Queen and her Henchman, from a bad performance of 'Snow White and the Seven Dwarves'.

'Now, young man,' said Mr Makepeace, 'how can I be of assistance?'

'Is there a back way out of here?' I said. It was half a joke, a bitter joke. I had no real hope of not being chewed up till the small hours of the morning. I might want to save Spartan. I might want to save Granda's house and things. But I was too weary and sick with misery. I hadn't even had time to say goodbye to Granda. Killed in a second by a hit-and-run driver outside his own cottage gate. Only sixty-seven. Full of life. He could've lived forever.

They'd yell and yell at me, and I'd do what they wanted. In the end. The bitter end.

'Yes, there's a back way out of here,' said Mr Makepeace. 'It comes out on the Totton road.'

Totton. Where Granda lives. Lived. Four winding country miles and you were there. Parking your bike at the white front gate. Walking up the brick path between the wallflowers. Granda opening the front door. Somehow he always spotted me coming. Spartan coiling round his legs . . .

Never again. Never ever again. Where *are* you, Granda?

'If I might suggest,' said Mr Makepeace respectfully, 'you should secure the cat, Spartan. A neighbour called Mrs Spivey is feeding him twice a day but . . . arrangements may have been made to dispose of him . . .'

I shot upright. The RSPCA might come at any moment. Black Spartan, sitting sunning himself on Granda's front doorstep, all trusting . . .

'Shall I phone for a taxi?' asked Mr Makepeace.

I ran my hands hopelessly through the pockets of my best, my only suit. 'I've got no money . . .'

'I am prepared to advance you something on account. I think that will be in order. Will a hundred pounds do? To be going on with?'

I looked at his nice old face. He twinkled at me; perhaps it was a trick he'd picked up from Granda. I reckoned he knew a lot about the way things were in our family. Granda must've talked to him.

He rang for the taxi, to wait on the Totton road. He got me to sign a few things, then unlocked an old tin box carefully and handed me a thin wad of new bluebacks, with the brown wrapper still round them. Then he gave me a thick stiff folded paper.

'Here's your copy of the will. You won't lose it, will you? And if there's any way I can help further, don't be afraid to give me a ring.' He shook hands, in a way that made me feel important. 'And remember, Master Tim, possession is nine points of the law . . .'

On the way downstairs, I took a quick look out of the staircase window, at the parental Merc parked outside. My mother and father were still yelling and waving their hands at each other, like two Great White Sharks saying grace before meat.

Then I ran all the way up the back lane. The taxi was waiting on the Totton road.

'Where to, Sunny Jim?' asked the elderly driver.

'Rose Cottage, Totton,' I said. 'I'm going to live with my grandfather. He's called Bill Wetherby.'

I paid off the taxi with the first of my wad of bluebacks, and just for a moment, it seemed true. His immaculate roses shone in the slanting sunlight. There was his spade, still stuck in the earth, at the end of a row of potatoes. His green watering hose was lying coiled on the brick path. And Spartan was sitting on the front doorstep, waiting. He rose, with the stately solemnity of a family butler, and came to greet me.

And then a voice behind me said, 'Is this the cat?'

Oh, it was the RSPCA all right. The official cap; the official van.

'This is *my* cat,' I said.

'I have instructions,' he said. 'This is Rose Cottage, isn't it? A black cat, answers to "Spartan"?'

I was glad to have the will, to shove in his face. I jabbed with my finger at the bit about Spartan. He didn't look very convinced, even when I'd finished.

'You look a bit young,' he said, doubtfully. So I showed him my driving licence, as proof of my identity. I told him to ring my lawyer, Mr Makepeace. But I couldn't shake him off. I looked about desperately for something to hit him with. A garden rake?

But just then Mrs Spivey came bustling over from across the road. I explained to her, and showed her the will.

'Put down *Spartan*?' she said in shocked tones. 'Old Spartan? That would've broken the good old boy's heart. Who's ordered such wickedness?'

The man consulted his paper. 'A Mrs Wetherby, of Alpotton.'

'That woman's a fool,' I said. 'A meddling trouble-maker. I know her well. A busybody. A troublemaking busybody.'

Mrs Spivey nodded emphatically to everything I said.

'She's not well liked in this village,' she added. 'Not at all well liked.'

The RSPCA man said, 'Wills – there's always trouble

131

about wills,' and finally went off, shaking his head dubiously.

Mrs Spivey looked at me. 'You shouldn'ta said that about your own mother, boy . . .'

'It's true,' I shouted a bit, still worked-up.

'It's true enough,' she said, stubbornly. 'But you shouldn'ta *said* it, that's all. You gotta live with her . . .'

'I *haven't*.' I shouted.

'What you goin' to do, then, boy?'

After she had given me the keys and gone, I let myself in, called Spartan in after me, and locked the front door and shot both the bolts. Then just stood in the hall, shivering violently.

The grandfather clock ticked on, soothingly. *He* must have wound that clock. The Sunday morning he died. Every Sunday morning in life he wound it, and set it right, because it lost three minutes a week. Soon, it would stop, and that would be like another death in the house. I couldn't *bear* it to stop. I took down the key from the shelf at the side of the dial, and wound up the great weights right to the top again.

It seemed a very good thing to do. Were there *other* good things to do? I didn't seem able to think at all; it suddenly hits you like that. I just stood and trembled; trembled and stood, watching the spots of light from the window crawl across the well-polished lino.

I might have stood there forever, if Spartan hadn't saved me. He came and asked for his dinner. He always gave that tiny miaow, so tiny in so huge a cat.

I went to the kitchen and fed him and watched him eat. Then it struck me it was time to feed the hens. The hens always got fed after Spartan. But it was a mucky job, and I was in my only decent suit.

A pair of Granda's bib-and-brace overalls were hanging on the back of the kitchen door. I took a deep breath, and took off my suit with a rush, and put on the overalls and his wellies and went and fed the hens. Then the pig. She's called Hettie; she's a breeding pig, and Granda's had her for ages. Granda sold her piglets for fattening, but he always swore Hettie would die in her stall, good old girl. And so she would! I scratched her back when she asked for it, and talked to her, as Granda did. She seemed glad to see me; she was lonely for him, like me.

There was a sense of peace and quiet in the fly-buzzing sunlight. I somehow knew Granda was there, watching. And that he was pleased with me, for feeding all his animals. I felt so much better; I even felt hungry for the first time in a week. I went and got some bacon rashers out of the fridge; a packet *he'd* opened. And a tin of beans off the shelf, and cooked them. Sat in his dungarees, and ate his food at his table. And it felt *great*. I felt so happy I burst out suddenly singing. One of his old songs. One by Sir Harry Lauder.

'Keep right on to the end of the road, keep right on to the end.
Though the way be long, let your heart be strong,
Keep right on round the bend.
Though you're tired and weary, still journey on
Till you come to your happy abode,
Where all you love and are dreaming of
Will be there at the end of the road.'

Then I burst out crying. Jesus, it's terrible having somebody die. You feel you're flying a plane through a thunderstorm with a load of crazy lunatics for passengers.

But old Spartan came and jumped on my knee, and reached up and licked the tears off my nose, as calm as anything. Then settled his huge bulk, with great care for his personal comfort. I stroked him, and it was better again.

It came to me, then, what Granda really wanted me to do. Just keep things running, as they had always been run. So that he could walk in any time, and find everything in its place. That seemed a most perfect ambition.

Then the telephone rang in the hall.

It was my mother.
'Oh, you're *there*. You've had us worried *sick*!'

133

'Sick enough for Dad to cancel his squash? Sick enough to cancel the Southwarks?' I really let her have it.

'Don't be offensive. We've cancelled *everybody*.'

'Tough shit!'

'When are you coming home? Daddy will come and fetch you.'

'Tell him not to waste his time. I'm staying here. Looking after things for Granda.'

'Don't be silly. You're going to university in six weeks' time!'

'I doubt it.'

'Have you taken leave of your senses? What about your future?'

'*Stuff* my future.'

'Don't be so silly. What're you going to live on?'

'Granda's money. He left me loads and loads and *loads*.'

He hadn't actually. Only about ten thousand in the Building Society. But no need to tell *her* that. Don't miss a chance to really screw her. She screws easy, where money's concerned.

'Listen to me. I am your mother . . .'

'I doubt it . . .'

There was a long, evil silence. Then she said, 'I think you've gone *mad*,' and hung up.

I gloated for a bit. Then a chill thought struck me. It would be right in their interests to get people to think I *was* mad. Then they could have me certified, and get control of everything again . . . Well, two could play at that game. I looked at my watch. Seven o'clock.

I rang Dr Marsden at his surgery. He'd been Granda's doctor. And another old mate of his. Got a gift of fresh eggs every week. Came to the funeral.

He told me to come straight down. I went. I knew I was safe for the night: my mother would be 'letting me sweat' as she would put it.

Dr Marsden was great. He let me pour it all out, without saying a word till I was finished.

Then he said, 'I don't think you're mad, old chap. Considering what you're going through. You're granda had a saying; it helped him a lot when he lost your grandma. He used to say, "You get a little stronger every day."'

'Yeah,' I said. 'That's sense.'

'Anyway,' he said, getting to his feet. 'Make sure you eat all right, and keep busy around the garden. There's probably a lot to do, it's a big garden . . . and see you get your sleep. If you can't get to sleep, come back and I *might* give you something. Come back and see me in a week anyway. Enjoyed the chat with you.'

He saw me to his gate. Sniffed the cooling air, and looked at the sunset. 'Going to be a fine day tomorrow.'

'Good night,' I said, feeling a lot better.

'Perhaps I shouldn't say this,' he added, and paused. Then he said, 'Your grandfather worried a lot about your father. And he worried more after your father married your mother. And he worried a lot about *you*. But I don't think he had much cause to worry about you. Good night.'

It was funny, when I got home. Spartan didn't come to meet me. I thought he'd gone out, because he didn't even come when I called. But when I blundered into the dusk of the kitchen, and banged the light on, he was sitting on the old rag-rug in front of the hearth. Staring at Granda's chair. Staring and staring. It was so . . . intense . . . I became convinced that Granda was sitting there. To tell you the truth, I didn't like that much. It's one thing to wish for people to come back; it's something else when they do. I mean, I couldn't see him, or hear him. The smell of him was strong, but maybe that was just the things in the kitchen cooling down after a hot day.

It was . . . unbearable. I couldn't *move*. But I couldn't go on standing there forever, or I'd have gone crazy.

It came down to, do I love Granda, or don't I? Alive or dead?

I couldn't bear not to love him. So I took a huge shuddering breath, and went and sat down in his chair.

It was strange. It was like sitting on Granda; it was a bit like sitting on his knee, when I was small. It was a bit like

Granda was a cool bath, and I was lowering myself into him. Or he was flooding into me, making us one.

I shuddered once more, and it was done. Maybe Granda and I became one.

Anyway, Spartan seemed pleased. He came and sat on my lap again, purring, the way he used to sit on Granda's lap, every evening.

I fell asleep with Spartan on my knee. And dreamed of Granda. He just walked in the door and I looked up and he grinned at me in his old way. And I said to him, 'Hey, I thought you were dead?' And he said, 'That's what they all think.' And we both laughed, and then he walked out the door again, to see to Hettie, and that was the end of the dream, and I wakened up with a crick in my neck.

It was ten o'clock. Time to go to bed. In Granda's bed, because mine wasn't made up, and I was too tired to start doing it now.

Spartan came with me, and curled up on the counterpane, in his old place, and it was OK.

I woke up about six, like I always do at Granda's. Because that's when he always got on the move in summer. Dazed, I listened for his stockinged feet creaking downstairs to make a mug of tea. Listened for that little cough he always had in the mornings, because he smoked.

Then it drearily dawned on me that I could lie there forever and there would never be creaking footsteps or that little cough again, and I made mysef get up.

But once I got washed I felt half-human and, as the doctor had forecast, it was the beginning of a smashing day, and there *was* a hell of a lot to do in the garden.

And, when Dracula and Mrs Dracula arrived, it would be best to meet them in the front garden, with the cottage doors locked behind me, and the keys hidden in the place that only me and Granda knew. That way, if they started shouting at me, as they were bound to end up doing, it would be in public, with half the village staring out of their windows, and that would soon put *them* to flight.

So after washing up the breakfast things, and last night's, I went out to the front garden, wearing Granda's wellies and dungarees, old collarless striped shirt and his old panama hat with the hole in the crown for good measure.

I started to work out where the old boy had got up to, the day he died. He'd been lifting his potatoes, to store in the little barn. And he would be dealing with the last of his broad beans by now, blanching the end of the crop for his freezer, and piling the haulms on to the bonfire-place for burning. I knew exactly what to do; I'd helped him enough as a kid.

I was well on, and sweating, when I heard the Merc draw up, near-silently, and the handbrake go on. I went on working, as if I'd heard nothing. My head was down, as I pulled out a potato plant and shook the soil off it, when I heard the gate creak. And then a rather loud gasp, that made me look up:

My father was standing there, clutching the gate with both hands, his knuckles white. His mouth was open, like a fish when you take it out of water. He was rather a nasty colour.

'Hello,' I said. 'You look like you've seen a ghost . . .'

And then it struck me, of course, that he had. I'm exactly the same tall thin build as Granda, and head down . . .

'Do you mind if I sit down?' he got out at last.

I nodded to the old white garden seat, with the ornate cast-iron ends. He sat down, and I sat down with him, because I was a bit worried, he was such a colour. And he didn't seem able to bring himself to say anything.

'Are you on your own?' I asked.

'Your mother's waiting in the car. I thought we might have a quiet word.'

Same old trick. In a crisis, my mother plays the tough bullying policeman, and my father plays the kind reasonable policeman. She's very good at it; he's not.

'We can't go on like this, Tim. It's not natural.'

'Yes, it is. You walked out on Granda. I walked out on you.'

He had the grace to flinch. 'Your granda and your mother didn't see eye to eye.'

'That makes two of us.'

'Tim, you don't understand. I was in the middle . . .'

'You didn't stay in the middle long. You walked out on him. You never came to see him. He was your *father*.'

'Tim, I couldn't stay here. I had my way to make in the world . . .'

'You made yours. I'll make mine.'

'But not going to university . . .'

'It won't sound good at Sunday drinkies, will it?' I said bitterly. 'It's one thing, saying your son's at university. Something else, saying your son's a farm labourer.'

'You wouldn't . . .'

'Bloody would.'

'You're *mad*. Your mother said it was no good trying to talk to you reasonably.'

'Well, she was right, then. For once. Run away and tell her I'm not coming home. Not for you. Not for her.'

He got up and stalked to the gate, all pseudo-dynamic. Then he sort of turned and crumpled, hanging on to the gate again. 'Tim, can't we talk this out sensibly?'

I suppose I was sorry for him.

'Not with *her* hanging around,' I said. 'Try coming on your own, sometime.'

He gave something between a grin and a flinch, and vanished behind my hedge. I didn't envy him, going back a failure.

I braced myself for the real onslaught. But it didn't come. In a few minutes, the Merc roared away, my mother driving. She shot me a look as she passed.

I was expecting the rage; I wasn't expecting the fear.

For the next few days, I just fell into Granda's rhythm. I'd been to see him so often, over so many years, that I seemed to know by heart what he'd be doing at any one time. Gathering the last of his greenhouse tomatoes, tying up the leaves of the cauliflowers so the heads didn't go green, dead-heading the roses. He had an old-fashioned cottage garden, that lovely mixture of flowers and vegetables. I even entered his stuff in the village show, and won quite a lot of prizes. All his doing; none of mine.

138

But people got to know that I was staying on. People started calling, to buy his eggs, to leave him the fresh-shot rabbits and little gifts of fruit they'd always left him. And I gave them the gifts he would have given them, in return.

Nobody in the village thought it strange I was living there. As far as they were concerned, it was Bill Wetherby's place, and quite right that his big grandson should inherit it. What else?

All through that glorious September, my old life faded. I did have the sense to write to my Cambridge college, telling my new tutor that I had inherited my grandfather's house and land, and was too busy seeing to them to go up that year. The tutor wrote me a very civilised letter back, saying I could only mature through being a working landowner for a bit, and to reapply next year if I wanted to. He couldn't have realised that Granda only had an acre of garden and an acre of orchard, and an acre of field for Hettie. But he did congratulate me on my A-level results . . .

But that was less important than the blackfly on the Brussels sprouts, which Arthur Digby pointed out, as he daily sat on Granda's white seat, and made sure I was doing things right. All the old boys in the village seemed set on that. I didn't mind. I wasn't lonely, I can tell you. I liked it, because they told me tales about Granda. How in the war he got dressed up in a white sheet and frightened the American airmen silly, as they lay in the hedgerows with the village girls. And about Spartan in his youth, when he bested the Alsatian guard-dog from the airfield.

I was even invited to join the Young Farmers Club . . .

Mother never came. But Dad dropped in once or twice. I took to keeping a few lagers in the fridge for him, and we sat on the seat in the front garden and drank them, and never found much to talk about, except how the turnips were doing.

'See yer dad was up last night,' old Arthur would say, the following morning. 'Us all said he'd never settle. Not like you've done, boy. You'll be thinking o' gettin wed, soon . . . ?

I never got a chance to get as settled as that, though.

It was one dusk early in October. I was pulling out couch grass and ground elder, keeping things tidy, working by the light of the open front door and the parlour window. Spartan was watching me closely, pouncing on the showers of soil as I pulled the weeds up. Then he gave a strange growl, and stared at the gate. Really, it made my hair stand on end. I looked up, expecting to see Granda standing there. You go on expecting things like that.

But there was nothing; only the sound of feet approaching down the village street. Female feet, and not village feet either. Quick nervous feet.

A tall woman looked over the gate; a stranger; I knew everybody now in the village.

I stood up and wiped the soil off my hands on Granda's dungarees. I was wearing my granda-set as usual.

She said, 'Oh, thank God, you're all right!'

'All right?' I was totally baffled.

'You're the man I nearly knocked down. In August. I just caught a glimpse of the dungarees and the hat as I passed you. Your hat fell off.'

'I wasn't here last August,' I said. 'That must have been my grandfather . . .'

'Is he all right?'

'No. He's dead.'

She gave a little cry, and clutched at the gate with both hands. I thought she was going to faint. So I said, 'You'd better come in. I'll get you a glass of water.'

I was half sorry for her; and half wanted to get her in, so I could ask her a lot more questions.

She sat down in Granda's chair, and I got her a glass of water, and she sat holding it, sipping it, and in between her teeth chattered. I'd never imagined that the hit-and-run driver could look like this. I had always imagined him to be some drunken young punk, somehow. Somebody who's teeth I could knock down his throat, if I ever caught up with him, which seemed unlikely.

140

'What happened?' she finally asked. 'To your grandfather?'

'He was knocked down by somebody who didn't stop, on the sixteenth of August at about five o'clock. Outside this house.'

'Oh, my God,' she said, and closed her eyes and clenched her hands so hard around the glass I thought it was going to break.

'What happened,' I asked, 'to you?'

'I was driving with my window open. A fly got in my eye and I swerved, and I thought I'd just missed a man in dungarees and a white hat like yours. There wasn't a bump or anything. So I just drove on. Then when we got home, my little daughter who was in the back said, 'The man in the white hat fell down.' There was nothing in the news. Or in the papers. But it's been preying on my mind ever since. In the end, I had to come back to make sure. All the way from Birmingham.'

'Well, you know now,' I said. Really hating her.

I wish I hadn't. Have you ever seen anyone go to pieces? Really go to pieces? Crying so you just can't stop them, no matter what you say, what you do? Being sick? I started off thinking about her going to prison, and I ended up thinking about her going to hospital.

She was quiet after a long time, just dragging in shuddering sobs.

And then Spartan, who had been sitting on the rug beside me did a damned funny thing. He made that odd growly noise again and leapt on her knee, and licked the tears off her nose. She clutched him, hugging him, her thin tense fingers chafing at his fur like she was almost strangling him. But he just purred and didn't seem to mind.

I knew it was Granda again. Granda forgiving her.

And if Granda forgave her, who was I to point the finger?

So I said, 'You didn't hit him much. He only had a little bruise on one knee. But you knocked him off balance and his head hit the kerb. The kerb killed him. If there'd been no kerb, he wouldn't have died.'

141

Her eyes stared at me so. 'I must go and tell the police.'

Something made me say, 'What's the point? He's dead, now. That won't bring him back. It wasn't your fault the fly got in your eye. Could've happened to anybody.' Anyway, I said it.

We sat a long time, after that. I told her all about Granda, and what a good old boy he'd been, and how everybody missed him. Then I told her a lot of stories about him, including the one where the hare jumped over his head in the harvest field.

And she cried for him. As my father hadn't cried. As my mother hadn't cried. That night was Granda's proper send-off, from the cottage; after the funeral.

Around ten, she rang up her husband, to say she would be staying the night, and we talked on till about two in the morning, making it a proper send-off. Then I showed her up to Granda's bed, and slept on the couch in the parlour.

In the morning, she gave me her address. If I ever changed my mind, she was willing to go to the police.

But I never changed my mind.

I spent the whole winter with my grandfather. Getting up in that dark and cold house; breaking the ice in the morning, in the kitchen sink. Reading late by the dying coals of the kitchen range. Feeding the chickens in the snow-covered field. Going up to bed with old Spartan.

And I spent the spring with him. Watching the stuff coming shooting up in his garden. He had planted some, and I'd planted some, and they came up together, and they were good.

And summer came in, and I began to worry about Spartan. Nothing you could put your finger on; but he was slower. He slept more, and ate less. He grew thin. I took him to the vet but the vet just looked at his teeth and asked how old he was.

I didn't know. Ever since I could remember, Spartan had been there.

'Nineteen's a good age for any cat,' said the vet. 'But